C. K. Williams has lived i.. ... Australia and Paris and is a regular visitor to ... not teaching creative writing at Bonn University, Willi... loves to cook (and bake). More often than not, you will be able to find Williams on a train flitting to and fro in Europe or the United Kingdom, realising once again that she has forgotten to bring lunch, and proceeding to buy all the croissants that live in Bruxelles Midi.

www.ckwilliams.eu

 twitter.com/ckwilliams13
facebook.com/ckwilliamswrites

Also by C. K. Williams

Flowers for the Dead

LOCAL WHISPERS

C. K. WILLIAMS

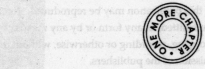

One More Chapter
a division of HarperCollins*Publishers*
1 London Bridge Street
London SE1 9GF
www.harpercollins.co.uk

HarperCollins*Publishers*
1st Floor, Watermarque Building, Ringsend Road
Dublin 4, Ireland

This paperback edition 2021
First published in Great Britain in ebook format
by HarperCollins*Publishers* 2021

A catalogue record of this book is available from the British Library

ISBN: 978-0-00-835442-8

This novel is entirely a work of fiction. The names, characters and
incidents portrayed in it are the work of the author's imagination. Any
resemblance to actual persons, living or dead, events or localities is
entirely coincidental.

Printed [and bound by CPI Group (UK) Ltd] [FS] Renewable Electricity
by CPI Group (UK) Ltd

To Chris and Lucy
Jolene and Leo
Gareth and Emma
And to my mum

Girls and boys, come out to play,
the moon doth shine as bright as day;
leave your supper, and leave your sleep,
And come with your playfellows into the street!
Old nursery rhyme

"It is the tree originally known as yew, though with other related trees becoming known, it may now be known as common yew, English yew, or European yew. Primarily grown as an ornamental, most parts of the plant are poisonous, and consumption of the foliage can result in death."
Wikipedia

Did you know?
The Romans believed that yews grew in hell.
The Woodland Trust

Let me drive you home, I say.

She shakes her head. I'm not scared, she tells me.

I laugh, my neck flushing. I didn't want to drive you because I thought you were scared.

Oh.

Oh, is all she says.

Right.

I lift both hands. No worries, I say.

No, listen, she says.

Let me get the bill, I say, trying to spare her the embarrassment of having to lie to me about all the ways in which she does not find me attractive.

No, she says fiercely, I am paying.

Let's just split it down the middle, I suggest.

She looks so relieved.

Were you really worried about that? I ask her a few minutes later, when the bill is lying between us on the table, both of us haphazardly throwing notes on top. Haphazardly in my case, anyway, attempting very hard to conceal my disappointment. She is watching closely, making sure I do not put down too much. Were you worried about me paying the bill? I ask.

She looks at me with an expression that I find impossible to read. Yes, she says simply, instead of lying or making up an excuse or laughing it off, and I like that. For the first time tonight, I feel like we are actually talking to each other.

Why? I ask. Outside, the sun has already set on Queen's Wharf. Outside the large glass windows, I can see the lights of Stockton on the other side of the harbour, the dark twisted lines of the old pump house and the concrete factory. It is warm out. It is summer in Australia. Everyone is already drunk. I work at a local hostel, reception and cleaning. The former gets me the minimum wage, which is very decent, the latter free board in a single room, more privacy than I have had in months. Which I thought to make the most of.

She is a guest at another hostel. We met at a backpacker party. She is from Belfast, I am from Gelsenkirchen, a city in Germany that she had never heard of and couldn't pronounce, and I thought this was going somewhere. I thought that was what she wanted.

Because there should be no expectations, she says.

Do men really expect you to sleep with them because they bought you dinner? I ask. It is that time of the night, three pints in, where you can suddenly say things you would not say during the day.

She looks at me carefully, this man having dinner with her, so clearly trying to get her into bed. She is taking measure.

If you wanted to stay for just one more drink, she says cautiously, I could tell you the story of three girls in a backpacker hostel up in Seventeen Seventy-Seven, three girls who had all slept with a man who had bought them two drinks.

Is it a true story? I ask.

The only ones worth telling, she replies.

All right. Was one of those girls you? I ask.

Are you staying for one more drink? she shoots back.

Do you want me to stay for one more drink?

Yes.

Why?

Because you asked. Because you want to know the truth.

I almost grin. That's all it takes? I ask. Could have saved myself the wining, the dining, the suit?

A smile pulls at the corner of her mouth. It looks mischievous. It is a look I like.

Oh no, she says. I very much like the suit.

Well then, I say. One more drink it is.

One drink turns into seven. Four of those in my room. At the end of the night, Kate and I are friends.

Breaking
01/01/2019 4:39 PM

COUNTY DOWN, NI: A YOUNG WOMAN, AGED 17, HAS BEEN FOUND DEAD IN HER PARENTS' HOME TODAY. THE POLICE HAVE TAKEN IN A SUSPECT FOR QUESTIONING. NO ARRESTS HAVE BEEN MADE AS OF THIS AFTERNOON.

Day 1

WEDNESDAY 2ND JANUARY 2019

Kate's voice is firm when she calls. "Can you come?"

It has been nineteen years since we met in an Australian hostel, and her voice still sounds exactly the same.

"Now?" I ask, voice raw with sleep, separated from her by roughly one thousand kilometres of landmass and ocean.

"I'm in police custody. A patient of mine was murdered yesterday." Her voice breaks then. "She was still a child."

I book myself onto the next flight to Belfast. Thank God for easyJet. On the way to Dortmund airport, I stop off at the agency and tell my partner. She assures me she can handle the campaigns on her own. Anna has always been like that. I tell her to call me should she need me, then I'm off. Everything takes too long. Especially passport control. Entry check, exit check. I wish Kate was living in Paris or Dublin or Warsaw or Rome, so long as it didn't oblige me to tell a border patrol officer that I was here for reasons of leisure.

"I was your phone call," I say, because there really isn't anything for me to do but state the blatantly obvious.

We are at Ardmore Police Station in Newry, a city only eight miles from the border with the South. The building is a fortress rather than a police station. Accessible only through heavy gates, rising up high on a hill, walls painted orange, every inch of it under constant surveillance. It could not be more different from the village where Kate lives if it tried, and Annacairn is more of a hamlet even than a village, thirty miles on winding country roads into the Mountains of Mourne. There on the grey slopes, where the old stone walls disappear into mist and twilight, on the very outskirts of the village, stands her small house with the old rowan and yew trees all around like a sacred grove of old.

But there are no facilities in Annacairn to hold someone who is a suspect in a murder investigation.

Kate is sitting across from me at a plastic table. She is wearing her own clothes, thank God, a smart suit, her red Italian. She would look just like herself, if there were still laces in her shoes.

"There is no right to a phone call under British law," she says. "There is no right to a visit, either."

"They let you phone me anyway," I say.

"I have the right to a notified person," she says. "You're my notified person."

I would like to reach out and take her hand in mine. But for some reason, I find that I'm not brave enough.

"What happened?" I ask.

Kate looks at me. We found her first grey hair the very night we met. It has been nineteen years, and her hair has gone entirely white. It suits her. It is bright and elegant and cannot be ignored, just like her.

"I don't know," she says. Her voice doesn't break until the very last word.

She reaches across the table. I hate that it was her who had to do that. I meet her halfway. Our fingers intertwine.

And then she tells me.

"I was due for a house call." Kate is trying to sound neutral. She is trying to give me a concise account, even when her voice is trembling.

"Where?" I ask gently.

"At the Walshes. Megan and Patrick Walsh. It wasn't them I went to see, though. I was there to see their daughter Alice. She's seventeen. Was. She was... seventeen. I've been their GP for years. Known her since she was a baby. Alice Walsh got all her vaccines from me, all her check-ups."

She swallows. Looks at our hands.

"I drove over there. Her parents weren't in, still at work. They have a house on Rostrevor Road. I got out and rang the doorbell. No one opened, but they leave the door unlocked, so I let myself in."

She takes a deep breath. "Anyway, the moment I stepped through the door, I smelled it."

And then she looks at me: "I smelled the blood, Jan. I know what great quantities of human blood smell like, from the maternity ward. I called out for Alice, but there was no reply. And then I checked. First on the ground floor. Then on the first. And the smell..."

She falls silent again. She has to look away. "She was lying on her bed. If you can call it that. She was..." She closes her eyes. "Her body parts had been severed from her body. Her legs, her arms, her hands, her fingers, her thighs and shins and feet. But each part had been arranged on the bed so that it seemed as if her body was whole. It took me a moment to…"

I can feel the horror rise even as she continues: "I cannot forget it. When I close my eyes, I… Her upper body was twisted. As if she'd tried to escape into the mattress. Her hips had been brought forward, and her head was turned towards the left. She was looking straight at me."

I press her hand more tightly. Kate looks back at me. "At first I didn't see the parts had been severed. I thought she was… whole. I rushed to her side. But there was nothing I could do, Jan. There wasn't. She was already dead. I knew that, even before I realised that someone had cut off all her limbs and each of her fingers and arranged them back together."

"You called the police?"

Kate nods, with difficulty. "And then they brought me in. Because they think I might have done it."

"It is a formality, isn't it?" I tell her. "You were the first at the scene of the crime."

She nods.

But she doesn't look convinced.

My heart stutters.

She doesn't look convinced.

I settle down at the station to wait. I take out my phone and read up on custody regulations in Northern Ireland. And here is one thing I never thought I would have to do.

Once I am done, I put my phone away. I sit in the plastic seat and look at the wall, glaringly white, freshly painted, offensively clean. I would go and wait outside, but there is a little snow on the ground, and snow reminds me of Kate. It was the first word I taught her to say in German, *Schnee*.

A couple of hours later, they release Kate on police bail. The Detective Sergeant informs us that the scene cordon at Kate's house has been lifted, and that Kate has to remain in Annacairn so that they will know where to find her. The Detective Sergeant is standing at the counter, watching us, glancing at the clock every now and again. A bag sits on her chair, a white cap and red gown peeking out, as if she was off to a fancy-dress party later tonight. I'm about to comment on it, that it looks just like the costumes from *The Handmaid's Tale*.

Then all I do is say goodbye.

"Let me drive," Kate says, when we walk up to my rental. She is clutching her shoelaces.

"You're not insured on this," I say carefully.

"You're not used to driving on the left," she proclaims, an utter falsehood. I always drive when I am here. I drove through all of Australia.

"Maybe it would be best if you just sat down and…" I start, but she interrupts.

15

"For fuck's sake, let me drive, Jan!"

Silently, I hand her the car keys. Kate unlocks the doors, sits down in the driver's seat. She toes off her shoes. There is a run in her tights. The line of her shoulders is brittle. "Would you fix my laces while we go?" she asks, doing her utmost to get herself back under control.

"I would be glad to," I reply quietly, taking the shoes off her with all the reverence they deserve before beginning my silent work. Kate drives down the busy main road, going past the rec ground opposite the station, surrounded by high fences, the small furniture shops further along the street, the giant Tesco Extra on our right, the one where we always go at least once to get our shopping when I come over. The Coop in Annacairn has household coal in large white sacks, a small post office, dog food, instant Lamlac and a bargain bucket as well as vapor refills, but it doesn't quite cover a week's shopping.

Kate leaves the town through suburbia, past more churches than I have seen anywhere else in my life except maybe Adelaide in Australia, and drives east into the mountains.

When she is out again on an open narrow road, hedges and trees rising to our left and right, the snow lying thick on the meadows where the sheep would be grazing, that is when she speaks up: "I'm sorry."

"Don't worry about it," I say.

"I shouldn't have snapped at you," she insists.

"I get it."

Kate glances at me. "Just because you're empathetic doesn't mean I get to behave like a dick."

I look back at her. There is a small smile curling up the corner of her mouth, even with all the lines of exhaustion marring her face. I smile back. Kate and I have always been excruciatingly honest with each other. I couldn't be friends with someone who wasn't. When you run an ad agency, you learn to crave candour.

Her expression softens. Her shoulders soften. Kate softens into that smile of mine, and I turn back to her shoes. "There," I say. "Good as new."

"Did you have a good flight?" Kate asks.

"Oh, is that right?" I ask, straightening the laces. "We're going to talk about my flight?"

"Has Ryanair started introducing stand-up tickets yet? Did you have to hold onto a railing at taxi, take-off and landing?"

"I flew easyJet," I say. "You've got to give these a polish, Kate, they look ludicrous."

"You are just jealous because my shoes are smarter than yours."

"Don't change the subject."

"My shoes aren't an appropriate subject for conversation, then?"

"Yes, because it will allow me to transition very elegantly into what I really want to talk about." I put her shoes down next to my feet, then turn to her. "How are you?"

"Wretched," Kate says, her knuckles white around the steering wheel.

I hesitate. I want to touch the back of her hand, just for a moment, watch how she relaxes her fingers. "Why did they suspect you, Kate?" I ask instead, clutching my hands together in my lap, now that we are in the safety of the car and driving ever deeper into the mountains.

"There were bloody clothes at my house. Of Alice Walsh's. She had gone through a... a medical procedure a few days ago. There were complications and she came to me for help, after hours, because she did not want her parents to know. That is why the clothes were there."

I stare at her.

Kate keeps looking straight ahead.

"Fuck," I say.

"Can we get drunk, Jan?" she asks, still staring at the road. "Can we get drunk and make carrot cake and black bacon and potato farls, and then can I break down crying, because I am so bloody scared?"

"Yes," I say.

"Aren't you going to ask me?"

Kate is looking at me in that way of hers as she asks, slurring her words a little. That way she has, where she's trying to look not into your eyes but right into your brain, your mind, your soul, should there be such a thing.

"Am I going to ask you what?" I ask, not sounding significantly more articulate than her. We are both on her sofa, my legs curled up under hers; we're older now than we were when we met, but our friendship hasn't changed, all brutal honesty and casual touching.

There's just something I haven't told her yet. Something she doesn't know about me.

Kate gestures with her glass. Fortunately, her Irish coffee does not spill. She's still in her suit after all, even though she has taken off the jacket and rolled up her shirtsleeves, while I am very comfortable in my pair of faded jeans and grey wool sweater. Her arms are thin and shaking, and her voice is loud and boisterous, like a fist in my face. "Aren't you going to ask if it was me?"

I pretend to think about it. Then I take another careless sip of my gin and tonic. "No."

She makes a face. She almost seems disappointed. I hide my smile behind the rim of my glass.

Then I realise that my drink is transparent.

"Why not?" Kate asks. There is a tremor to her voice, a wary vulnerability and unguarded hope that very nearly breaks my heart. "They seemed to have reason enough to suspect me."

"Do you want me to suspect you?" I ask.

"No," she says. "Absolutely not."

"Good. Because I would like to ask you a different question. Two, actually. Did the police believe what you told them about the bloody clothes?"

She rubs her eyes. She never wears make-up. The suits are her only extravagance. "I'm not sure. I don't know if I would, to be honest."

She looks at me. Then she looks to the side. "What's the second question?"

"Have they taken anyone else in?"

"I wouldn't know. Why?"

"You did not do it," I say. "But Alice Walsh is dead. So who did it?"

Kate shivers. The ball of her foot is digging into my leg. I want to reach down, rub the soles of her feet. Instead I reach for the last slice of carrot cake sitting on the coffee table. Right there, next to the bowl of chips, sits the pan containing the veggie sausages that we served still sizzling, and most importantly, the potato bread. Whenever I come back here, all I want to eat is potato bread. You can't find it anywhere else, not like this.

"Jan, you should have seen her," she says quietly. "I can't imagine that anyone could have done such a thing."

"It is usually a partner or ex-partner or close family member, when the victim is a woman," I say. My sister's a detective. She'd be a much bigger help to Kate now, I can't help but think.

She shakes her head. "No one in Annacairn... I just... I don't believe..."

She peters out. Then she looks back up at me: "And yet, somebody did."

That is when her doorbell rings.

Kate's eyes flicker to the sitting-room door. She's struggling to speak. There is an expression on her face that I cannot interpret, so rarely have I seen it there. "Can you..."

She stops herself.

"What?" I ask, eager to do anything for her. Needing to be needed. It's so easy, living life when you are needed.

"No, never mind."

She makes to rise. I put my hand on her foot then. Her skin is cold under mine. "Kate."

She closes her eyes for a moment.

"Would you go and open the door?" she asks, and she can't look at me while she does, and then I know what that expression on her face is.

She is scared.

"Of course," I say gently.

While I rise, while I leave the sitting room and go out into her hall and towards the front door, I cannot help but think that there is fuck all I could do if a murderer turned up at our door. I'm the creative head at an ad agency who hasn't worked out properly in a long, long time.

It's only when I have put my hand to the door handle that I realise my fingers are shaking. Kate rarely shows when she is scared. When she does, there is good reason to be.

It's too late. I am already opening the door.

Coming face to face with a man I don't know.

He is taller than me, which is not such a feat, albeit very thin. No belly on him, not like mine. There is something about my body that is soft, while he is all angles. He may be my age, a little younger perhaps, although it is difficult to tell. He is dressed in a black suit, wearing a clerical collar. Its white tab is almost blinding against the dark that lies outside the house, where you can see nothing but the outline of trees and hear nothing except the whisper of the wind sneaking through sharp branches and old granite stones.

"Good evening," he says. His voice is soft. It rumbles. There is an accent. Scottish as far as I can tell. And yet, there is a hitch to it. Maybe he is surprised to see a strange man standing in Kate's doorway. He certainly looks me up and down, before quickly focusing back on my face. "I am here to see Kate."

"Let me just check if she's... if she wants to... Let me just check with her," I say. My tongue fumbles with the words. It always takes a couple of days, finding my way back into it, especially with strangers, back into the language I only ever speak when I am here, once or a twice a year when I come to see Kate, or to myself, alone in the flat or on the subway pretending to be on the phone, when I miss the taste and shape and sound of English too much. The ease with which it allows me to utter things I would never say out loud in German.

I return to Kate, who is still holding onto a chip. "It's a priest," I tell her, not bothering to hide my surprise, unlike him. As far as I am aware, Kate isn't religious. At least not practising, much like myself.

"Oh," she says, dropping the chip back into the bowl. Her neck is flushing.

I furrow my brow. The way she looks at all the food spread out on the table, the bottle of gin that sits half empty next to the ravaged cake. "Would you mind just straightening things up a little?" she asks, avoiding my gaze as she pulls down her sleeves, even doing up the buttons at the wrist.

"Worried what he'll think of you, committing the sin of gluttony with me?" I ask, trying for a light tone of voice.

Her eyes find mine, just for a moment. "Maybe," she says. Then she disappears into the hall.

I get the distinct impression that there is something she isn't telling me.

I take the plates, bowls, bottles into the kitchen and start covering them up with a tea towel, which surely counts as straightening things. I cock my ears, trying to hear them talk in the hall.

"I'm sorry to be coming by at this hour," the priest says. "I didn't know you had a guest."

"You know about Jannis," Kate says.

"I just wanted to let you know that everyone is coming together at the church. For a vigil. For Alice. I wanted you to know that you're very welcome there."

"Am I?" I hear her ask. Hear the tension in her voice as I put our glasses into the sink, as quietly as humanly possible.

"Kate," the priest replies. "Of course you are. Of course.

It's ludicrous, that the police... I want to make sure you know this. That's why I want you to join us."

There is a moment's hesitation, then Kate speaks, and her voice sounds small: "I'm not sure, Dan."

"Don't be silly, Kate," he says, just as quietly.

Then there are noises I cannot place. Maybe he is taking her into his arms.

And finally, Kate speaks up again.

"Yes. All right. I'll be there."

We've both technically had too much to drink to be driving. Kate says she's feeling fine, however, and it is true, she hasn't had as much as me. I would never do this at home, but here, the rules seem to be just a little different, and I'm strangely content to follow along.

"Have you known him long?" I ask when I'm back in the passenger seat of my rental, dressed in my warmest coat, and still my teeth feel like chattering.

"Daniel?" Kate replies, as if it wasn't painfully obvious whom I was talking about.

"If that's the name of the priest."

"A few years," she says, going for careless.

"In a religious capacity?" I try.

She laughs. "God, no."

"How does he feel about your blasphemising?" I ask, not about to let her get away with her monosyllabic answers.

"That's not a word," she says, not looking at me. "And he doesn't give a shit. He's the same age as us, he's not like the priests from our childhood."

"What's the right word?"

"What?" Finally, she glances at me.

"What is the right verb for blasphemising?" I ask.

"As a good Catholic girl, I'm happy to let you know it's blaspheming."

Kate slows down as the church comes into view. There is a long line of cars already parked on the side of the road, and she pulls up behind them. It's a church from a time when there were more than a few dozen houses inhabited in Annacairn; built of sturdy grey stone, with three sharp towers and glass-stained windows which look black in the night and yellow and red during the day.

As soon as she has parked the car, we go out into the cold. Kate buries her hands in the pockets of her coat. It's long and elegant and grey, definitely a little too light for a fresh winter evening with all the stars bright and cold in the sky.

"Aren't you cold?" I ask her.

"Nope," she says.

"You sure? You can have my ja—"

"You worry too much," she interrupts. "Pay me a compliment about my coat. It's new and I've seen you look at it."

And she is so right. We have a thing about clothes, she and I. "Style over substance, huh?" I ask her, tugging at her coat. She pulls it out of my grasp but manages to look a little pleased with herself. "But great fucking style, am I right?"

I nod, and we are both grinning as we walk through the gate and up to the church.

It is only when Kate pulls open the door that her face falls again.

Everyone seems to have come. Black shapes under the dark arches lit only by candles. Some kneeling, some sitting, some standing or pacing. At the very back stands a large group of sobbing teenagers, who I suppose are Alice Walsh's classmates. It is only when we walk past them that they fall silent. The air is thick and unmoving. We walk up the aisle. Kate stares straight ahead. I glance at the pews. There are some faces I vaguely recognise; faces I may have once known but that have changed beyond recognition; faces that do not ring a bell at all. There is a decided lack of anyone under twenty, except for the teenagers at the back and two strangers sitting in the front pew, a young woman and a young man, roughly the same age as Alice Walsh. He is crying, she is holding him. He is in black skinny jeans and a matching sweater, the garment far too thin for this time of the year. She is wearing a black long skirt and an even longer scarf. She looks fierce. He does not.

"Alice's parents aren't here," Kate mumbles, scanning the congregation as we approach the altar. I have to suppress the instinct to cross myself. Instead, I keep observing the congregation as we turn to the left and make for the devotional area. I don't know what I was expecting, maybe anger, maybe outrage, accusations, or even endless tears, grief waiting to turn into rage. But the young man and Alice Walsh's classmates seem to be the only ones who are crying. All other displays of grief are curiously contained. And the teenagers at the back are almost too noisy now that they have started sobbing again.

There is something off about this. No one is quite capable of meeting our eyes, no one except Daniel, who comes rushing over when he spots us.

"Thank you for coming," he says quietly, as if Kate was a perfect stranger. Now he's trying a little too hard to be casual. He is trying so hard, in fact, that it suddenly occurs to me they might be sleeping with each other.

If he weren't a priest, that is.

Another man comes up to join us. He was one of the group by the votive. A man in his early thirties, head shaved and eyes bright blue and dressed only in a sweater in spite of the cold. Sean O'Doherty, if I remember correctly. A policeman, I believe, though not a detective. CRC, maybe, crowd and riot control? I don't believe that we've ever been properly introduced. I've only seen him from afar, when he was pointed out to me by Kate. A few years back, I suspected her to be a little smitten with him, but I don't know if anything ever came of it.

"Kate," Sean O'Doherty says sharply by way of greeting. "Did they treat you well in custody?" Not one to beat around the bush, it seems. "The Murder folks are a weird bunch."

"They were all right," Kate says. "Just doing their job."

"Fucking wankers is what they are."

"Sean," Daniel says, a quiet admonishment.

Sean raises his eyebrows. "Tess and Elizabeth are smoking, Father," he points out, indicating the two women with a sharp movement of his head.

I look at them. I remember Tessa Adams well; she drove the only bus, on the days that it went, until she retired; she's standing a little further down the wall, wearing her customary heavy boots and flimsy cardigan. Her mother, Elizabeth Adams, who I've never spoken to, is sitting in a pew with her legs crossed and a cigarette holder. She is an endlessly elegant lady in her early eighties, wearing a floor-length black dress and a few pearl necklaces and a ring with a bright green stone. From what Kate told me, she's a unionist and spent the better part of the early Nineties refusing to speak to her son.

Her son, William O'Rawe, who is just now coming walking past us, his wife on his arm, both of them doing their utmost to ignore us. They had been standing with Father Daniel by the votive before. William O'Rawe is a tall man in his late fifties, highly attractive in a Robert Downey Junior kind of way, dark hair turned dashingly grey, a finely groomed beard and fashionable glasses. Next to him is Florence O'Rawe, with her wide brown eyes and long curly hair, who runs the library cart and wears floral dresses no matter the season. They are both staunch republicans. A deep rift runs through that family, from what I have gathered over the years. Even now, William O'Rawe seems to be walking over to his mother. He points at her cigarette, as vocal about his disapproval as Sean is.

"They need something to hold onto?" Daniel tries, watching Elizabeth Adams ignore her son and keep smoking.

"Did they tell you why they were taking you in?" Sean

O'Doherty asks Kate. "They have to, you know they do, don't you?"

"I'd rather not talk about it right now, Sean," Kate says.

"Course not," Sean says. "Let me know whenever you're ready. I'm already asking around if anyone saw a car they didn't know, or a stranger after nightfall or loitering somewhere during the day, all that."

"Would that not be best left to the police?" Daniel asks.

"I am the police," Sean says with a distinct note of pride.

"You're riot control," Kate points out.

That was not what Sean wanted to hear. "Do you have somewhere you can stay?" he asks Kate.

"My house?" she replies.

Sean's expression turns unhappy. "All on your own?"

"If you need a place to stay, the rectory has a perfectly cosy guest room," Daniel says. His voice is shaking a little, and his smile is tender, not simply friendly.

Kate shakes her head, sounding bemused. "All I want is to go to sleep in my own bed, Father."

"Let me drive you at least, Kitty," Sean says.

"I can drive," Kate says. There is some steel in her voice.

"I know you can," Sean says. "It's just that I don't want you going home on your own. It might be dangerous."

"If you keep an eye on the church later, Sean, I can drive her," Daniel suggests.

"Nobody's driving me," Kate says sharply.

"You shouldn't be on your own, I agree with Sean," Daniel repeats. "None of us should be alone tonight."

I take a step forward. "I'm staying with Kate," I say.

Now it's Daniel's turn to look unhappy, whereas Sean's

expression brightens. He extends his hand: "Didn't see you there. Sean. O'Doherty. Police."

I shake it. "Jannis. Advertising."

Sean grins. "Like Janice Joplin?"

"First time I've heard that joke," I answer, not losing the smile. Of course, my name is not actually pronounced anything like Janice, but I've gotten used to it.

Sean claps me on the shoulder. "It's fine, not your fault your parents gave you a girl's name."

I decide not to correct him.

"See," Kate says to Daniel, "perfectly safe," going for a smile, then interrupting herself, putting on a serious expression instead. She seems lost. Such a strong woman, lost. "I'd just like to light a candle," she finally says.

I veer off towards the statue of St Brigid while Kate moves over to the votives. Leaning against the wall, a little way down from Tessa, I reach for my phone, checking if Anna has texted, if the meeting went well.

There does not seem to be any signal in the church, however. I put the phone away and go back to observing the congregation. There's something very odd about this gathering. The stillness.

Then I catch sight of something. There is a long thin object leaning against the wall right opposite me. I squint. It looks very much like a rifle.

Since when were rifles allowed into a church?

Noises from the front pew. The young man and the young woman. They have risen to their feet. He is still clinging to her. "I am so sorry," he whispers, but it resounds in the quiet church. "I'm so sorry, Betha."

31

What has that young man to be sorry for, then?

Something appears in my line of sight.

A cigarette.

"Want one?"

It's Tessa's arm, stretched out towards me. She is still looking straight ahead, but I'm the only one she is currently offering a fresh cigarette to, so she must be talking to me. "I don't think that we're supposed to," I say quietly.

"Didn't think you'd be the guy to care."

Well. If she would like to picture me as some sort of devil-may-care rake, who am I to object?

I take the proffered cigarette, glancing at the door, but the young couple has already left. Expecting Tessa to hand me a lighter next, I stretch out my hand, but all she does is pass me her cigarette. I light my own on the tip of hers.

"We shouldn't, really," I say, even as I inhale the first drag. Sort of shattering the James Dean impression, I am sure.

"Well, they shouldn't have murdered a seventeen-year-old girl, but they didn't give a damn, did they?"

I take another drag. It has been a while. This isn't the first time that I have come back to the nicotine after promising myself I was finished with it for good, so I already know what to expect. The acrid taste, and the smell even worse. "This really isn't very nice, is it?" I ask her, lifting the cigarette so that she knows what I'm talking about.

"No, not really," Tessa answers. We are speaking in low voices. "I just needed something to do. To make me look upset. Figured smoking in a church would do it."

I stare at her. At her yellow cardigan, the dotted green blouse, the jeans worn high around her waist. Her face, the lipstick on her mouth and the deep lines on the back of her hands and throat. "You aren't upset, then?"

"Of course I'm bloody upset," she says. I can see her swallow. "But it's not enough, feeling it, is it? They've got to see it, too."

She motions at the people in the pews, by the votives. I lift the cigarette back to my lips, even though the taste is beginning to make me feel sick. "Is that so?"

"Course it is. Take yourself, for example. You wanna know what they've been saying about you ever since it got out that you've flown all this way to bail her out?"

She looks at me shrewdly.

"I can barely contain my curiosity," I say, not taking another drag.

"That you and Kate are fucking. Must have been for years, actually."

I can feel a thin smile cross my face. What I want to say is: have they not noticed she is sleeping with their priest, then? But I am much better at keeping secrets than His Holiness. Besides, she is making me angry. You see, Kate has been nothing but a pillar to this community ever since she moved here. I didn't get it, being a city kid, how she could move out here, into the middle of nowhere, no matter how beautiful the scenery. But she wanted to help. She said, I studied medicine to help those who need it. I'll go where no other doctor wants to go.

And this is what she gets in return? "I get it," I reply,

perhaps a bit more hotly than I should have. "Life in the countryside must be so boring."

If Tessa was hoping to startle me into a confession one way or another, she doesn't let it show. I look at my cigarette. Consider stubbing it out against the soles of my shoes. Then I realise I am no longer twenty-two and my shoes are a little too expensive, really, to serve as ash trays. Tessa sighs and lifts her own leg, worn rubber boots.

"I couldn't," I say.

"Can't stand on one leg for very long," she informs me.

"Fine," I say, pushing out the cigarette against her boot. Her stance is sturdy.

"Listen," Tessa says. "Just a piece of advice, 'cause you never got on my nerves with a lot of chitchat when I'd had to drive you somewhere. Sure, dismiss this, that's up to you. But people see you and think you're on her side. And she was the one the police found with Alice Walsh's bloody clothes. That's all I'm saying."

I start. It does not escape her. Still those shrewd eyes are on me. "Didn't tell you that, did she?"

I say nothing. Of course she did. I just don't know how this information got out, and I don't like that it did. Not one little bit.

Now they're suspecting her, too?

Kate? Kate of all people?

Before I can ask any more questions, Kate is coming over to join us. "Tessa," she says, but Tessa interrupts her before she can say any more: "Don't ask about the bloody hip."

Kate lifts both hands to placate her, smiling again. She cannot help it, it seems. "It's my job," Kate says.

"Be a GP in your practice," Tessa says. "Or am I asking if you want a single or a return ticket? And stop smiling, love."

Kate wipes all traces of mirth from her face. No matter that Kate and I are in our forties, to Tessa we will always be brats. Tessa puts out her own cigarette. "Well, no hard feelings, kids, but I'll go stand over there."

And then she simply leaves us standing there. Goes to join her mother, eighty-one years old, and put an arm around her shoulder. Elizabeth most decidedly does not look as if she needed an arm around her shoulder. Instead, she looks at Kate with an expression of such righteous contempt that I almost recoil.

Kate glances at me, then asks under her breath: "Did she just run away from me?"

"And advised me to do the same," I say. "Apparently, everybody is saying that you and I have been sleeping together for the past nineteen years, and that you murdered Alice Walsh and I helped you hide the body."

Kate isn't very good at hiding her emotions. Her expression immediately twists into one of poorly veiled fury.

"I know you said you didn't care what they thought," I say "But Kate, why is an eighty-one-year old lady staring at you as if she would be happy to see you burn at a stake? No, don't look," I add, but it is too late, Kate has already turned towards Elizabeth.

Kate's face falls even further. She looks so very exhausted. In a way that she didn't when we were younger.

"Do you want to go home?" I ask.

"Aye," she says, shaking her head. "Let's just... Maybe..." She glances at me. "Maybe say a prayer before we go?"

I am almost ready to gape at her. Then I close my mouth again and nod, offering her my arm. We walk to a pew further towards the back, closer to the entrance, evading at least some of the curious glances. I slide into the pew first, then kneel.

"Our Father?" Kate asks.

"A classic," I say, and then we both start whispering the words. Even though it has been years, it is so easy, even comforting to fall back into the script. To go through the motions, to fold my hands just so and close my eyes and bring back the words. Words that are here for me, without even having to think about them, without having to work for them. She says them in English while I speak them in German. It's the same with Disney songs; whatever I learned at an early age in German I tend not to know how to say in English. So I hear her speak next to me, the familiar lilt of her voice a calming presence in the oppressive silence. "Our Father who art in heaven, hallowed be thy name..."

While I speak the same words in another language, "*Vater unser im Himmel, geheiligt werde dein Name...*"

And then I have to think of Alice Walsh. I don't know whether she was religious. Whether she believed in an afterlife. Did she even think about death yet? I remember the moment I realised that I would have to die one day, and it was not at seventeen. At seventeen, I still felt invincible.

To my right, I hear the sound of the church doors

opening once more. I keep murmuring the words to the prayer even while I glance to my left, towards the door.

It is not the young couple.

"It's Alice's parents," Kate whispers. She must have looked up, too.

The silence that descends is so heavy. I watch them as Kate and I start over with the Lord's Prayer. Patrick Walsh, of whom I know only that he became a father so late in life, who is seventy years old now by Kate's report but looks ninety-nine. His narrow face and high cheekbones and thin skin, a man as slim and tall as a birch who spent all his life working on construction sites. And Megan Walsh, small but stout, always dressed in cardigans for as long as I've come here, blue in the winter, green in the summer, a woman who watches all the rugby matches in the pub, gets happily drunk and then shouts at the players, alternating between telling them to get a fucking move on and how bloody hot they are. Kate told me she laughed all the time when she fell pregnant at forty-one and would tell everyone who wanted to hear it that hers was closer to a miracle pregnancy than even the Virgin Mary's.

Father Daniel is meeting them in front of the altar. Sean is with them, so are William and Florence O'Rawe. They speak in low voices.

Then Megan Walsh turns to look straight at us.

Her stare makes my blood freeze.

Then she turns back to Father Daniel, and it looks as if she may be hissing at him. Father Daniel looks incredibly uncomfortable, as if he is valiantly trying to talk her out of something. Sean O'Doherty's feet are firmly planted behind

Megan, an arm around her shoulder. Patrick Walsh is standing off to the side, openly crying, facing not the altar but one of the narrow stained-glass windows. William O'Rawe is standing by his side, trying to offer comfort. They go way back, if I remember correctly. Rumour has it they go back far enough to have been in the IRA together.

I watch Daniel's shoulders slump. He begins making his way towards us. Slowly, I rise to my feet. There is something about the way he moves. In this church and its stark shadows cut into slices by flickering strips of candlelight, it almost looks like there is a demon coming down the aisle.

I meet him at the end of the pew. His expression is full of discomfort.

"I need a word with Kate," he says, trying for a collected tone, but there is more to his voice than sorrow. There is also anger.

Interesting.

"She's praying," I say.

"What are you, her bodyguard?" he asks.

My eyebrows shoot up. He takes a deep breath. Looks down. It seems as if he is actually ashamed of himself. For losing control.

And suddenly, it physically hurts how much I can relate to that.

"What's the matter, Father?" I ask, gentler than either of us expected.

"I'd much rather tell her," he says.

"I bet you'd much rather not tell her at all," I say.

He gives me a pained smile.

"They want us to go, don't they?" I ask.

He nods.

My chest constricts. I step out of the pew, to let him in to talk to Kate. As I move past him, I realise that his thin body is thrumming with suppressed energy. For no more than a moment, I close my eyes and enjoy the sensation.

Then Daniel moves into the pew and sits down next to Kate. He lets her have a few more moments, then he gently touches her shoulder. She looks up. The tender smile he gives her almost makes me jealous. I cannot remember when the last time was that anyone looked at me with anything akin to love.

Then Daniel leans in close to speak with Kate. I watch her face fall. She glances at Patrick and Megan Walsh, but neither of them is looking our way anymore.

Sean O'Doherty is, though. And the slim veneer of concern has vanished entirely from his expression. I wonder if the news of Alice Walsh's bloody clothing has only just reached him.

I stand a little taller, just to make sure he sees. "You coming, Kate?" I ask.

Kate nods. She trails after me as we leave the church. I'm relieved to get out of here. Churches are so quiet. So heavy. They are crammed with memories, stacked so tightly I hardly find any space to squeeze through. Knobbly knees on the pews, the scent of incense in my hair and clothes, a boy faced with boredom and silence and oppression. Rules on all sides, like the pews, sitting for them standing for them kneeling for them.

We're silent as we get into the car. She starts the engine

and pulls out into the road, leaving North on Moyad Road to go to her house that sits on the very edge of Annacairn, in a last stretch of tall dark trees before the slopes of the mountains turn naked and bare. The land once used to belong to Elizabeth Adams's family, before they had to sell it off, and with her house two miles off, on the other side of the wood, the old woman is still the closest neighbour.

We've headed down the road for a mile or two and one of us has yet to say a word. Since Kate has had a nightmare of a day, I take the duty upon myself: "Are you sleeping with the priest?"

That shocks Kate out of her sulking. "Man, you have no tact."

"I don't know whether to find it amusing or infuriating how he is trying and failing to be subtle about it."

"Well, he isn't really supposed to, is he?" she says, focusing back on the road. "Vows of chastity and all that. I try to comfort him when I tell him that studies have shown that 80 per cent of priests had broken their vows of celibacy on at least one occasion, and that 40 per cent of priests are sexually active, if you include sex with both men and women."

"Is that so?" I ask, surprised.

"There was an article in the *Telegraph*," she replies. "There was the case of Father Mossy back in the late 2000s, and the case of a bishop ten years before. I mean, it isn't surprising, is it? Did you know that priests and nuns, living like husband and wife, is known unofficially as the third way in the Church? They preach compulsory celibacy, but very few are living it."

"And is this something Daniel takes lightly?" I ask her. "His oath of celibacy?"

She looks even more exhausted then. "No," she says quietly. "Actually, not at all."

"Poor sod." I am still looking at Kate. "Is it true love, then?"

Kate closes her eyes for a moment.

"Kate, the road," I say urgently. She opens them again.

"Not so much, I guess," she answers.

"Does he know this?" I ask. "Or is he of the impression that it is?"

"I've had enough interrogations for one day, Jannis."

"I didn't mean for it to be an interrogation. I'm trying to find out whether I need to be nice to him even though I don't feel like it."

That startles a laugh out of her. I knew it would, which is why I said it. "Doesn't hurt to be nice, Jan."

"Ah, but it's less fun. You should try it, too."

Some of the tension drains from her shoulders. "I actually should. God, can you believe those fuckers?" She seems torn between amused exasperation and real anger. "Did you see how Sean and Dan rounded on me in there?"

I do my very best impression of Daniel's dulcet tones. "You could stay at mine, Kate, it's much safer. A beautiful parish guest room, and have I told you of the conveniently large double bed that they were kind enough to put in…"

I make her laugh. She shoves me into the passenger door. "It doesn't hurt to be nice, Kate," I mock whine.

She laughs even harder. "He just wanted to get me to come home with him, didn't he?"

"No, I am sure he was truly worried about you," I say determinedly. "Just like Sean."

"Don't do the voice," Kate says, but she is grinning, and it is too late to stop me, anyway.

"You shouldn't be on your own, Kate, you shouldn't, no no, you need someone to protect you. You need me. I'm a riot police officer. I control riots. And murderers. And your every move!"

I can see she has almost given in to bursting out laughing. Instead, she raises a challenging eyebrow at me: "And what about you, Mister I'm-staying-with-her?"

"I'm staying with you. It's just the truth!"

"Well, would you have let me go home alone if you hadn't been?"

I furrow my brow, staring at her. "It isn't up to me what you do, Kate."

That puts a smile on her face. "Well, I'm glad you are here, anyway."

I relax into the seat, take my eyes off the road. Instead I look at her. "Are you worried?" I ask her quietly. "About your safety? Is that why you called me?"

"I don't want to be," Kate answers. Her eyes are still fixed to the road. There is something in her eyes. Something haunted. "But I am."

"Turn right here," I say, following a sudden impulse.

"Don't tell me what to do," she says automatically, but her foot has already moved, the car slowing down, her hands hitting the indicator.

"Let's go to Spelga Dam."

"It'll be dark and cold."

"There will be stars."

She glances at me, contrary even as she turns. "Want to give them fodder for their gossip?"

But she goes past her house in the small wood on our left, and keeps going further into the mountains, further up Moyad Road. The slopes of the mountains are rising on our left and our right, black masses in the dark of night.

The stars are clear and bright in the sky. We sit in the car in the parking lot just in front of Spelga Dam, watching the black water of the lake spread out in front of us through the windshield. There is a bench on the left side of the parking lot, right by its shore, where we have often sat whenever I come over in the summer. It has been covered in plastic foil, tied firmly with orange rubber bands, to protect the wood against the winter. The snow lies thick on the ground. Usually, it doesn't stay. Not for this long, anyway, and only very high up.

I know this place well. So well that it feels like home. On the other side of the water is the Magic Hill, where we have spent at least as much time as on the bench; it's a small stretch of road, and when you put the car into neutral, it will start reversing up the hill, all on its own.

The fairies push it up the hill. That is what everyone says around here.

I am from a post-industrialised mining town with an unemployment rate of 20 per cent. We don't have Fairy Hills.

All the happier are my memories of coming here with Kate. Of the Magic Hill and the Silent Valley and this parking lot with the picnic tables, transformed with the money of the European Union Regional Development Fund, the same money that has been paying for the campaign for the Mourne Mountains to become the first National Park in

Northern Ireland. I always joked about it. My tax money, refurbishing your private national park in Northern Ireland.

The water is impossibly black, lying calm and dark in front of us. And above it, there are the stars.

"Do you know how many fond memories I have of just sitting next to you in this car?" I ask her softly.

Kate is looking at the stars. Her eyes are glistening. She nods.

"The police will catch whoever did this," I tell her quietly but firmly.

She nods. "Oh, I know. After all, you have to have faith in the system, right? Otherwise you become a conspiracy theorist. I am not a conspiracy theorist." She smiles. Trying to make a joke even as her voice cracks. "Vapour trails really are used by governments to keep us docile; I'm just saying it how it is."

"Shh," I say, shifting closer, so that my shoulder is brushing up against hers.

"Sorry for this mess," she adds, still trying to laugh.

"It's not your fault," I say firmly.

"It was me who called you."

"I forbid you to beat yourself up about this," I say, not brooking any arguments. "I am glad to be here. And I will be even gladder to finish off that bottle of gin once we get back to yours."

"Shouldn't be driving, probably, should I?" she asks.

"No, you fucking shouldn't, but you never listen to me," I say.

Kate laughs. A real one this time. "Can't believe I'm

smiling," she says. And her voice changes again. "When I found her, I thought I'd never smile again."

I lean in even closer. "The dead would prefer us to smile."

"We can't know that."

"Believe my lies," I say.

"Gladly," Kate says.

And in the dark of the car, she leans her head against my shoulder. In the dark and silence, she starts crying.

It is pitch black when we return to her house, the headlights cutting through the darkness like pale ghosts. We are both laughing when we get out of the car, about something stupid, something we are laughing at not because it's funny but because we're tired, and that is a good enough reason. And when I glance at Kate as we go in and see her smile at me and hear that she is humming softly, it gives me hope that she will come out of this whole.

So we enter, her humming and me smiling and each leaning into the other, shoulders brushing, both swaying.

"You, cups," Kate says as she stumbles towards the sitting room.

"Tumblers?" I suggest as I toe off my shoes, attempting to save at least a shred of our dignity, but all I hear in response from the sitting room is an indignant "if you don't hurry up I'll have it out of the fucking flower vase."

So much for dignity.

I make my way into the kitchen, lights still turned off. I'd know where to go in this house with my eyes closed. I push the kitchen door open and step inside. Fumble for the next best set of glasses, which I decide is the two tumblers I'd put into the sink before we left for the vigil.

I pick them back up in the dark, throw my coat over the back of a kitchen chair, then return to the sitting room.

We drink some more. We talk. About anything but a woman cut into pieces and her bloody clothes in Kate's possession. We watch an episode of *Broadchurch*, because we

49

are both fans, until I realise this might not be too grand of an idea, so I yawn. And so does Kate.

"Let's go to bed," I suggest. "Things will look different in the morning."

So I return the tumblers and the booze to the kitchen. Kate calls out for me from the sitting room, moving into the hall: "I'm still re-doing the guest room. You don't mind sharing, do you?"

"When have I ever?" I call back. Then yawn again. I crack all the bones in my hands and pop my back, then I shuffle out of the kitchen and into the hall. She peeks her head out of the bathroom and throws a towel at me.

"Mind if I'm the first in the bathroom?" she asks.

"I don't think that I can stop you," I say.

"You know," she says, "I'm actually too tired to think up a witty parry. Be out in a second."

She closes the bathroom door as I make for the bedroom.

It is when I walk past the front door that I step on something.

It is flat, and thin. It feels like a letter, or a piece of paper. We must have not realised it was there when we came in just now, trampling across it still wearing our shoes.

Automatically, I bend down to pick it up.

My fingertips stop just as they come into contact with the paper. It is thick. It is cool. It is heavy.

That is when it occurs to me.

That this is not likely to be a regular mail delivery.

The one who sins is the one who will die.

Day 2

THURSDAY 3RD JANUARY 2019

NEIGHBOURHOOD PROTECTION

PROTECT YOUR NEIGHBOURHOOD
At Neighbourhood Protection we believe in partnership between the local communities and the police (Policing and Community Safety Partnerships (PCSPs)). We help you protect YOURSELF, we help you protect YOUR property, we help reduce YOUR fear of crime in YOUR community.

FIND OUT MORE...
Sean O'Doherty, Rostrevor Rd
Sodsodsod67@hotmail.com

Protect our neighbourhood!
PROTECT OUR WOMEN!!

The following morning, we are back in my rental and on our way to Ardmore Station in Newry. I'm driving this time, meadows and stone walls passing us left and right. In the spring, there will be wild daffodils growing everywhere and the yellow gorse in full bloom. It's my favourite season in these mountains, when they become so very cheerful.

They are not cheerful right now. There are multiple signs as we drive into Newry announcing, "We buy houses FAST". Beyond it another sign mounted on a trailer: "DANCE LESSONS NEWRY" with times and places posted in red letters below. Kate is calling her team from the passenger seat, to let her know that the practice cannot open today after the Christmas break as they had originally planned. The letter I found last night in her house is sitting in her lap, sealed carefully in a zip bag. It is only a thin slip of paper with black letters printed onto it.

The one who sins is the one who will die.

As I drive and she speaks to her assistant, I can feel that Kate is shaking. I wish it was with righteous fury. But one look at her face tells me that it is with fear. Fear she is trying to bury under fury. We pass by more signs, hand-painted, stuck to the streetlamps: "It is time to meet your maker". As we come closer to the station, this is followed up by "Prepare to meet thy God".

At Kate's request, I drop her off at the station and then

look for somewhere to park the car, finally settling for leaving it in the lot of the Tesco Extra. By the time I've made it to the station, Kate is already coming rushing back out, her face set in a grim expression. It can't have been more than twenty minutes. She snatches the car keys from my hands.

"Don't even think about it," she says as I open my mouth to suggest that I should really be the one driving.

"You can't keep taking it out on the rental," I say.

"I can try."

"It won't help."

"Well, neither will they."

"Did they say that?"

"As good as. You know what happened the first time I received threats?" she says, barging on towards the car. "They said there was nothing they could do until there was something more. Actual physical violence, for example. They did look very apologetic, too."

"You received threats?" I ask, angry with the police and shocked as I hurry to keep up with her. "When? And why are you only telling me now?"

"I wrote an op-ed for the *Irish News* when the Republic legalised abortion last year in May," she says, fumbling with the keys as we reach the car, but too upset to work them properly. "Daring to tell the truth, namely that women in the North are already aborting with pills you can order online, but they then can't legally go see a doctor for follow-up treatment, which some of them urgently need, and that it was time that the law recognised the reality and made it possible for women to seek medical help without the fear of prosecution."

Finally, she manages to unlock the car. "You know, I keep forgetting that abortion is still illegal in Northern Ireland," I say as we get in. "It always takes me right back to the 1950s."

"You weren't alive in the 1950s."

"Spiritually," I say.

"As long as you wear suspenders. Man, suspenders would look great on you."

This is how I know Kate. Always falling back on humour to defuse a tense situation. And we're both angry at the moment. She's angry with the police, and I'm angry on her behalf.

"What sort of threats did you receive?" I ask.

Kate starts the engine. "You are a baby killer, I will put you in hell where you belong, RIP. Quoting here, of course."

I squint at the road as she takes off, a little too fast if you ask me. "Not very consistent that. Rest in peace or rot in hell, what's it going to be?"

She laughs grimly. "I should have returned that witty reply. If only the threat hadn't been anonymous."

"I did not know that that you had received death threats," I say quietly. Kate, who doesn't have an evil bone in her body.

"It was only a few," she says, taking a sharp left turn with aplomb. "I showed it to the editor, of course. She said, honey, you should see my inbox. Rape threats, death threats, you name it, she's got it. I told the police, but this still isn't taken seriously, and you know what, as much as I'd like to blame the police, because old habits die hard, it's actually the politicians that won't legislate against online hatred and provide the necessary resources to law enforcement..."

She peters out. Eases up on the accelerator a little as well. I cannot quite hide my relief. "Do you often go on rage drives?" I ask as matter-of-factly as I can.

"Sometimes," she answers, truthfully.

"They are dangerous, as I am sure you do not need me to point out."

"So what? You're dangerous. I'm dangerous. I kill babies, remember?"

I look at her with what I hope is an appropriately chiding expression. I am still angry. This won't stand. They won't help? Fine. Then I'll have to.

"Show me the other threats. If the police won't help, we should look into it. Make a list of everyone who'd have reason to threaten you."

Kate nods. "Most of the threats were e-mails. I think I deleted those."

"Anything on social media? Any mail? Anything indicating that somebody knew where you lived?"

"There were a couple of letters. They're back at the house. I'll show you."

We are sitting on the floor in Kate's sitting room, breakfasting on cold veggie sausages and potato bread. I have hooked my phone up to her speakers and put on what I like to call French electro hip hop and what she calls "your noise". She has spread out the threatening letters on the coffee table. It is significantly more than "a couple".

"So, just eleven weirdos who found out your address and sent you death threats," I say, doing my utmost to stay calm. "Or one individual who's really determined. Nothing to worry about, you're perfectly right."

She elbows me. It actually hurts. "What good would it do me to worry? What was I supposed to do, shut my trap and never say anything in public again?"

"Well, no, but this is vile stuff," I say, rubbing my side. "That actually hurt, do you know that?"

"Well, getting called a cunt and a sinner hurt, too, but if I'd let it get to me, they'd have won, so I decided not to be scared of a few dickhead trolls."

"Almost a dozen," I say, staring at the letters. "Or, again, the same person." The contents are fairly generic, as far as death threats go. To be exact, two of them are death threats, three are rape threats, and the remaining six hit the sweet spot of combining the two. Generic isn't good. Generic means that any chance of tracing it to a particular individual, slim to start out with, is next to nothing. "Is there anything in these letters that struck you as particularly personal?" I ask her.

"I don't know, maybe the one that wanted to repeatedly ram a sharpened wooden cross up my vagina?" she asks.

"I meant personal in the sense that you had the impression that the sender may know you. You personally," I say, trying to stop my mind from conjuring up a mental image of what she's just described. I don't succeed. My insides are churning. I'm feeling nauseous. To imagine Kate like this, Kate of all people. She has always fought for those who are not given a voice, or proper medical care.

That she'd be threatened.

Kate looks back at the letters.

"Well," she says, pointing at the fourth letter from the top, "I remember thinking back then that this one was a little odd. Different from the others."

Both of us lean closer.

I shall take up your ridiculous scalpel and drive it right through the walls of your vagina, again and again, and then I shall cut your throat you cunt

"For fuck's sake," I say.

"Aye," is all Kate says. I see her press her legs closer together.

"The scalpel may simply be a reference to your profession?"

"GPs do not have a lot of reason to use scalpels," she points out.

"Which this stupid piece of shit may not have taken the time to think about," I reply.

"I know," she says. "It's just that I keep a scalpel in the

office. In the glass cabinet. The cabinet's locked, of course, but the scalpel is pretty prominent. It's the one Mum and Dad gave to me after I'd passed all my second MB exams. Bit premature that, but they were so proud. First person in the family to go to uni. It has my name engraved on it and everything, so I kept it. It may be a reference to that."

I look at the letter again. "It is interesting, isn't it," I say, "that they write 'your ridiculous scalpel'. Implies that they may be referring to a specific one rather than the generalised scalpel of the medical profession."

We both look back at the letters. "So, a patient?" I ask, reaching across the table for the white sheet of paper right in the centre. "Is it a patient we need to add to the list?"

We inspect the list. Which, at this point, is no more than a row of bullet points with names beside them.

"I still think Patrick and Megan Walsh should be at the very top of it," I say. "They kicked you out of a church."

"No," Kate says. "There's no way. Alice Walsh has been my patient all her life. I've been their family doctor ever since she was born."

"If your being someone's family doctor is our criterion for not putting people on this, there will not be a single name on here, Kate." I sit forward. "They mentioned your scalpel. It might be one of your patients."

"We could put abortion trolls on it," she points out.

"We've got to do something, Kate," I say. "These people are threatening you. We can't just sit here. Or did you call me so that I'd just be here and hold your hand?"

That riles her into action. "That'll be the day I die when we just sit here holding hands," she says, reaching for a pen, turning the sheet of paper around and beginning to write down a fresh list. You see, I know her very well.

"Okay," she says. "Okay, let's put them down. They'll be the first names, very top of the list."

She writes down on the first line, "Megan Walsh", and below it, "Patrick Walsh".

"Feminism, or order of likelihood?" I ask.

"Pat's so gentle. Even his voice is gentle," she says. "Order of likelihood."

"Men are more likely than women to commit crime," I point out. My sister is always keen to remind me.

"Not men like Pat," she says determinedly. "Who else should go on here, Detective Loser?"

I've already realised that Kate does not think that that joke will ever get old. My last name, I should point out, is Loose. Which in German makes perfect sense and has absolutely nothing to do with the word loser.

"How long have you been sleeping with Daniel?" I ask her.

"Dan? He is the gentlest soul I've ever met! Sometimes he's even too…"

"Kate, stop, the poor bloke." I can feel my face grow hot once more. I hope she doesn't notice. I haven't exactly told her yet. That I fancy blokes, too. "When did you start sleeping with him? Was it before or after you wrote the op-ed?"

She breathes out. "Before."

"Did his behaviour towards you change after it was published?"

"No!"

I say nothing. The most effective way to make people cave is to simply let them talk. Give them just enough rope to hang themselves.

"I don't know," she finally admits, wrapping her arms around her legs, her hands around the bare soles of her feet. She is still wearing the chipped remains of her Christmas nail polish on her toes, one nail red, the next white, the next green, and so on. The sight makes my heart seize. She has worn these colours all her life for Christmas, or as long as I have known her. "He's difficult to read sometimes, Dan is. Sometimes he looks at me in this way that makes me think he wants something from me, something I can't give him, and that that makes him angry. But he wouldn't send me death threats."

"Do you love him?" I ask.

She hesitates. "You know, I do not think it is love that he is looking for from me in those moments. It must be difficult for him. He so clearly feels guilty."

"But do you?" I ask. "Look for love from him, I mean? Or would it be better to break it off?"

She puts her forehead to her knee. "I'm giving this a try," she says. "Forty is no age to be picky."

"Jesus, thank you for giving me that outlook," I say.

"It's different for you," she reassures me. "You have that silver fox thing going for you, the ladies find it very dashing."

I shift. The ladies, yes. This would be an opportune moment, wouldn't it? To tell her.

"Is that really true?" I ask instead, looking at her chipped nail polish, at the second toe just a little longer than her big one, at her slim strong feet, much like Achilles must have had. "Do men really only want to be with twenty-year-olds?"

"You tell me," she says.

I tilt my head. Look back at the letters.

"I feel we should put Daniel on the list just to make sure we clear him," I say. "For women, partners or ex-partners are the most likely culprit, so we should just make sure there aren't any grievances there that we do not know about."

I can feel her looking at me. "Sure, put him down," she says. "It isn't like you to avoid a question like that, though."

"I thought you were being rhetorical," I answer. "I have yet to meet a man who would not like to sleep with a twenty-year-old. That doesn't mean that you want to grow old with them."

She lets it go. "What about Sean, then?" she asks.

"What about Sean?" I ask.

"Well, we dated."

"You dated Sean-the-riot-police-officer?" I ask. "See, I did think that you had a thing for him! Why do I not know about any of this?"

"It was only for a bit!" Kate defends herself. Yes, she is actually defensive. From what I have seen of Sean, I can't blame her. He is not likely to cloud my judgement, is all I'm saying. "A couple of years ago. Just thought I should let you know, because you said ex-partners."

"Quite right," I say, scribbling down Daniel's and Sean's names. "Why did you date him, though?"

Kate looks even more embarrassed now. "I wanted sex,

and I wanted it regularly, and he can be very sweet when he wants to be."

"He's a chauvinist," I point out.

"A pig," she answers miserably. "Can you believe it, he guilt-tripped me about being a vegetarian? He said it was offensive to him as someone who ate meat?"

"A chauvinist pig," I say, adding Sean's name to the list, which now consists of:

Megan Walsh
Patrick Walsh
Father Daniel
Sean O'Doherty
a patient?

"Anyone else that you can think of?" I ask. "It might be further back than a couple of years. Someone who has always held a grudge against you but needed an occasion to really have a go at you."

Kate leans back against the sofa. Her feet stretch out beneath the table. She could have been a dancer. She was quite passionate about it for a while if, by her own account, not very good. It is hard to believe. "I'm just a doctor," she says, a little helplessly. "I help people."

"Any patients who might have had the impression that you did not do right by them? What with the oddly specific scalpel reference?" I ask.

She stretches her arms, then crosses them behind her head. "I didn't do right by all of them."

I put the pen down. That isn't how I know Kate at all.

She is conscientious. She cares about everyone, always goes the extra mile. Whether a patient, a friend, a date, a neighbour, Kate would drop anything in an instant whenever somebody needs her help. Which is why this is making me so furious. "Anything in particular that comes to mind?"

From the corner of my eye, I see that she turns her head towards me. I could swear she lets out a relieved breath when she finds that she is not being scrutinised. "You make mistakes. That's just how it is. Sometimes people get that. Others don't."

I sigh and lean back myself, still looking straight ahead. "Kate, you are being unusually cryptic."

"I've been shouted at," she says. She does not sound angry, or like it might be unfair. "I've been insulted, I've been sued, but whenever I really messed up, when people actually had something to reproach me with, they didn't."

"Are you sure?"

"Well." Kate is drawing patterns on the floor. "Elizabeth Adams wasn't thrilled with me. This was quite a few years back. It's silly, actually. It wasn't even about her. Florence had come to me and asked about fertility issues, because she and William never managed to conceive. I referred her to a specialist, but just made sure to tell her it was essential that she took William with her to the appointment, because it was possible that it was him who was the issue."

"Elizabeth Adams felt personally insulted?" I ask.

"She threatened libel," Kate says, rolling her eyes. "It was a bad time for her. She'd just been diagnosed with senile depression."

"And what about William? Did he take it personally?"

She shrugs. "I never spoke to him about it. I don't even know if they ever went for any treatment. Nothing came of it, Jan."

"Still, just to be sure," I say, adding William O'Rawe's name to the list. "And there was nothing else?" I ask.

Kate stays silent. For a long while, all I can hear is the music in the background, one of my favourite pieces, a fast beat and a note of melancholy and words that I love the sound of even though I only understand half of them. Much like seeing a Shakespeare show at the Globe. Although I have not been to London for a while. When I come to the UK, it is usually to see Kate.

It gets to the point that I feel I have to look at her now, just to make sure she hasn't dozed off or gone away to some place in her mind where I cannot follow.

It turns out that she is looking straight at me. Her expression is a bit painful. "You're not going to like this," she says.

"I presume that is not because it has peppers in it," I say with as straight a face as I can. I have an intense dislike of peppers, as she well knows.

"Jan, wind your neck in."

"Just tell me."

She bites her lip. She looks flustered. Actually flustered. "So, um, you know how I said that Megan Walsh and Patrick Walsh, I've been their family doctor for ever and all that?"

"You are right," I say drily, "I am not going to like this."

She elbows me again.

"Ouch, you really have to stop doing that!" I complain.

"So," she says, "this must have been a few years ago, because Alice Walsh had only just gotten her period. I think she was twelve. She left school in the middle of the day and came to my practice. Catholic all-girl school, no one you'd want to talk to there."

She grins at that, but it is a grim one.

"Speaking from experience?" I ask carefully. I have always wondered at many things in Northern Ireland. How deeply religious education still is, is one of them. Just the thought of education segregated by gender seems to me to hail from another age, even though it is not as long ago as all that. My parents still went to segregated schools, my mother in Hamburg, my father in Dortmund.

"You bet your arse I am," she says, making a gesture which she aborts mid-motion, as if reaching for her breast pocket. This is where she used to keep her cigarettes, I know. The movement pushes me back into the past for just a moment, both of us sitting on the same floor up against the same sofa, wildly drunk and smoking and trying to outshout each other in a karaoke match of John Farnham's genius power ballad "You're the Voice".

"It's ludicrous, twenty years on, and Alice Walsh still doesn't have anyone to talk to at school about her period when it happens," Kate says, bringing me back to the present. "Anyway, so she came down to the practice and talked to me. I gave her pads and showed her how tampons work. This was before menstruation cups became a thing. Not that they're everybody's thing, obviously. There's a lot of fuss being made about the cups, isn't there?"

70

She looks at me expectantly. All I can do is shrug. Kate rolls her eyes. "Sure, you think this doesn't concern you. Period, women's business."

"How did I turn into the enemy here?"

"It's not you, it's the patriarchy, so it is. Anyway, I basically told her it was all right, it was a perfectly normal thing to happen, asked her how she was feeling, asked her about any pain, gave her a blister of Buscopan, told her she could come back any time if she had any questions. Turns out she had a lot of questions."

She leans towards me. I lean towards her. I cannot fathom what Alice Walsh would have had questions about that Kate needs to whisper about. Kate leans even closer. "About sex."

"About sex?" I ask, taken by surprise. "Right, that would be normal, wouldn't it?"

"See," she says, throwing her hand up triumphantly. "That's what I said! But anyway, so, she had questions about sex. Sex ed at her school had been completely useless. But she'd already started having sexual experiences, according to what she told me, so it was high time someone educated her. So I told her about contraception and about pregnancy risk and STDs and masturbation, that it was good to know what you like, about consent, too, and then I talked about LGBTQ for a bit. And I also mentioned the clitoris."

"Outrage," I say.

"You should have seen her, Jan," she says. "I told her that it was all normal, what she was going through. Just gave her some basic information. By the time she left, there was an actual spring in her step. Just the relief of having someone to talk to. Who doesn't like it when people tell you that you're normal?"

"Right," I say, suddenly uncomfortable. How nice indeed when someone can tell you that what you feel is normal. "I suppose it's a bit like when you ejaculate for the first time as a boy."

She peers at me. "What was that like?"

"Let's not get into one of the most embarrassing moments in my life, which sadly involved not a medical professional, but first my eye-rolling mother, and then my flustered father, and then, again, my no-nonsense mother and a very strange homemade picture book," I say. "What happened next?"

Kate turns fully towards me, drawing her knees back up to her chest, her eyes wide. "I don't think anything of it, right? I just watch her go and am happy I could help. But that evening, just as I'm closing up, Megan Walsh comes to my practice."

"And I suppose she didn't come to thank you for what you had done for her daughter?"

"Fuck no. She was livid, Jan. She wasn't just shouting. I thought she was inches away from strangling me at one point."

I turn towards as her as well. "What was her problem?"

Kate almost shrugs. She laughs, the laugh of the helpless, the baffled. "God wanted us to be abstinent, I'd turn her daughter into a slut, hell was a real place."

"Hell was a real place?" My eyebrows must be somewhere in my hairline at this point.

"Don't quote me on this, but I remember there being frequent mentions of hell."

"Okay," I say.

"They wouldn't, though," Kate says. She's staring off into the distance. "They've just lost their daughter. I haven't even been able to tell them how sorry I am."

She presses her lips together. Then she rises to her feet. The threatening letter is still lying on the table between us. "I will write them a card." She extends her hand and pulls me to my feet.

"Are you sure this is a good idea?"

"We will just put it through the letter box," she says. "They won't even know we were there."

Patrick and Megan Walsh live in a nice grey stone house which looks to have been recently built or refurbished. Out on Rostrevor Road, their house is surrounded by meadows where sheep are undertaking an unsuccessful attempt at grazing. And always the mountains, grey slopes fading into the fog, and the clouds, ancient stone walls forming black blurry lines, slowly disappearing into the grey mass of heavy snow and the pale sky.

We park the car and get out. It is cold, the wind biting sharply at our skin, my hair. It is often windy here, but the weather is also bound to change quickly. We are so close to the sea, only a few miles to the south. The Mourne Mountains are beautiful, their slopes and woods reaching right up to the coast. Whenever I come here, they make me think that they are the perfect melange of Scandinavian fjords, pine trees from Southern France, and the epic mountainside. It is both a disgrace and a stroke of luck that no one really seems to have heard of them yet. Unless they watched *Game of Thrones*. I watch the lonely road vanish into the shreds of clouds climbing across the tops of the mountains, snaking their long pale fingers down the slopes and into the valleys, reaching for the dim grey houses, shivering in the rain.

A notice catches my eye. Someone has put up a hastily drawn poster of sorts on the mailbox.

NEIGHBOURHOOD PROTECTION

PROTECT YOUR NEIGHBOURHOOD
At Neighbourhood Protection we believe in partnership
between the local communities and the police (Policing
and Community Safety Partnerships (PCSPs)). We help
you protect YOURSELF, we help you protect YOUR
property, we help reduce YOUR fear of crime in YOUR
community.

FIND OUT MORE...
Sean O'Doherty, Rostrevor Rd
Sodsodsod67@hotmail.com

Protect our neighbourhood!
PROTECT OUR WOMEN!!

I glance at Kate, but she has already walked up to the door. She takes a deep breath. Then she puts her card through the door.

"All right?" I ask her.

She nods.

"Let's go, then," I say gently.

We have not reached the car again when the front door is suddenly opened.

Patrick Walsh is standing on a doormat spelling out WELCOME, holding Kate's card, looking terribly frail. Even more so in the bright light of an unforgiving day.

"Patrick," Kate says. "Sorry, I... I just wanted to..." She

peters out. Then, rallying her courage: "I am so sorry for your loss."

His blue eyes look down at the card in his hands. "The police advised us not to talk to you."

Kate's back is ramrod straight. "It's... Pat, you must know that I'd never, never..."

Patrick Walsh's eyes well up. It happens so quickly, Kate does not even have time to finish her sentence. He starts crying.

"Pat," Kate takes a step towards him, then stops. Pat wipes his eyes.

"Meg's coming downstairs, Kate. We're off to the graveyard, they're putting up a ... a thing, a cross, a memorial of sorts, seeing as we cannot have the body yet... You'd better go."

"All right," Kate says. "Of course. Sorry. We'll be off." Patrick Walsh closes the door. Again we turn to the car.

"The poor man," Kate says. She seems shaken to the core. "The poor man."

Just then, the front door is thrown open once more.

"How dare you?"

This time, it is Megan Walsh standing in the doorway. She is wearing her blue cardigan. She is wearing red lipstick. "How dare you come here, you bitch?"

Intuitively, I step in front of Kate.

"Come on, Kate," I say and open the car door for her. "Let's go."

"If you ever come back here again, I'll kill you," Megan Walsh says. She is not listening to her husband, who is trying to hold her back. She is not shouting, either. No. Her voice is eerily calm. "You better get out of this town, Kate. I don't ever want to see you again. I'll make you regret it if you don't."

"Meg," her husband says, "Meg, please…"

She turns to her husband. "Stop crying. Just stop crying."

He doesn't.

"We have to go," she goes on. "You have to stop, Pat, because we have to go to the graveyard, and we cannot fall apart."

"What are you doing at the graveyard?" Kate asks quietly. "Will there be—"

"Don't you dare show up there," Megan says. "Don't you dare. I'll fucking kill you if you do."

And all of a sudden, Kate looks like a small girl that someone has dressed in a suit.

12:12

Kate, back in the passenger seat and thank God for that, reaches for her breast pocket again. No cigarettes. It irks her that I saw. She pouts at my admonishing glance.

Then she puts her feet up on the dashboard.

Then she drops her forehead to her knees. "Drive me to the church?"

"Kate," I say, once more doing my utmost to stay calm and reasonable. "She made it perfectly clear that she doesn't want you there."

She turns her head to the side. Looks at me. "Not to the graveyard. To the church. I want to see Daniel."

The graveyard sits to the left of the church, old headstones spreading out across a hill covered in snow, the mountains rising grey and shapeless in the background. An ancient yew tree grows at the crest of the hill, its limbs as thick as battering rams of old. I took a class on the Classics at university. Greek Religion. In Ancient Greece, yews were considered to be the tree of Hecate, the liberator of souls after death. The roots of Hecate's yew tree grow into the mouths of the dead so that they may remove the soul.

The Romans looked at it a little differently, I think. They thought the yew tree grew in hell.

That is how Christian culture came to associate yew trees with death.

Crows are rising from the nearby fields as I park the car. We get out and make for the church gates through the thick white snow. They are made of old wood, carved with leaves and spirits and demons. There is a monstrous Jeep parked in front of them, and Sean is leaning against it as casually as a drug dealer. There are more of those posters everywhere. NEIGHBOURHOOD PROTECTION. Sean flips away his cigarette. Kate looks at it longingly, I disapprovingly. If there is one thing I cannot abide, it is littering. Kate glances at me and knows exactly what that expression on my face is.

"You dropped something," I point out as graciously as I can.

Sean does not pay me any attention. "Sorry, Kitty," he says. He even looks it.

"About what?" she asks.

"Come on," he says, physically barring her path. "You know they don't want you here."

"I'm here to see Daniel."

He shrugs. "Well, you can't. He's got better things to do."

She glances over her shoulder. "Just let me through, Sean. I don't want to be here when Meg and Pat arrive. They've just lost their daughter. I'm the one who found her. They don't need to see me standing here."

"That's right," Sean says. "So piss off."

Kate swallows hard. "You don't think I did anything to her, do you? You can't think that, Sean. You know me. I'd never hurt anyone, I've sworn an oath—"

"Well, you don't take that one too seriously, do you?" Sean interrupts.

"What do you mean?" she asks.

"You think killing babies is okay," he says.

"Woah," I say, "all right, let's calm down, everyone."

"Do me a favour, stay out of this," Sean says, his sharp blue eyes suddenly focused on me. "This is none of your business."

"Come on, Kate," I say. "Let's go. You can call Daniel once we're home."

But Sean steps up to me. I can feel his breath on my face when he speaks. "You staying with her, eh? Funny timing, isn't it?"

"Back off," I say. He is ten years younger than me and lifts twice as much weight at least. I have no doubt that he'd love to punch me, Sean would.

"Listen, buddy," Sean says. "None of this is any of your business. Go back to where you came from. Take her with you while you're at it."

"Dan!" Kate calls out just then.

Steps on the gravel. Sean looks over my shoulder, then takes a step back. I risk a glance over my shoulder, wondering who managed to make Mr Riot Police cower.

It is Father Daniel striding towards us. He looks very tall and very thin, his expression stormy, and I am reminded of the impression he made on me in the church last night. A demon rather than an angel.

"Oi," he says. "Break it up, whatever this is. Meg and Pat will be here any moment."

"Exactly," Sean says defensively. "Seeing Kate is the last thing they need right now."

"Is that your cigarette butt?" Daniel asks. "Would you mind not littering my churchyard?"

Grumbling, Sean bends down to pick up his cigarette butt. It is fascinating to realise that Daniel is an authority figure. Sean holds onto the butt with an expression of distaste. He looks around, presumably for a rubbish bin. Kate rolls her eyes and takes a small metal box out of her bag. I made her carry that around while she was smoking, because I could not stand it when she would drop her litter everywhere. Funny that she would still have it with her.

Sean looks darkly at the proffered box before he drops the cigarette into it. "Happy?" he asks Daniel, who has come to stand between Sean and me.

"Do I look happy?" Daniel asks, and no, he does not. "If Kate wants to speak to me, she can speak to me."

Sean raises his brows. "You picking her side?"

"Kate is part of my congregation," Daniel says sharply.

Sean presses his lips together. He is evidently fighting some internal battle. When he speaks, the words sound a little pained: "I'm afraid that isn't only up to you, Father. I'm the Neighbourhood Protection Co-ordinator, and I think that it isn't safe for her to come to the church currently. She is the only suspect the police have taken in so far, after all."

Something passes across Daniel's face. "Is that what you think, Sean?" he asks. His voice is quiet. An unpractised observer might take this to mean that he is intimidated, but that is not what I see. I see a man who is saying it quietly to give Sean the opportunity to change his tune without losing face.

I see a man who is ready to make Sean change his tune.

Suddenly, I am concerned for this strange, thin priest who would not hold out one second against Sean. Not that I could necessarily hold my own for much longer, but at least my body shape roughly matches his.

"It's not what I think. It's what I'm doing," Sean says. Give a man like him a measure of power and he's going to make the most of it. He turns back to Kate. "I'm sorry, but it's my responsibility to keep this community safe. That's the most important thing. I don't want you to come back here. In fact, I think you should leave for a bit."

Daniel takes a step towards Sean. Before I have time to think about it, my arm has shot out, wrapped around his wrist, to hold him back, although all I want to do is hit Sean myself. "Calm down, everyone."

Daniel looks at me. More specifically, my hand on his

arm. For a moment, his expression stays absolutely blank, almost as if he was in shock.

I let him go immediately.

"It's all right," Kate says. "I'll call you, Dan." Then she sweeps past us, returning to the car. I follow her quickly.

The whiskey bottle is back out and French electro hip hop back on. Our feet are bare and cold in the sitting room. Kate is swaying to the music. So am I. She is an intensely elegant creature when she dances, so much so that everything about her seems heightened, changed. If she turned her back to me, I might not even recognise her.

The less said about my dancing the better.

After a couple of songs, I am on the sofa, rethinking that knee surgery that Kate claims I need and that I refuse to consider before I have turned forty. Kate is sitting next to me. We are both breathing heavily.

"Do they really believe it?," she asks suddenly, quietly.

"Believe what?" I ask.

"That it was me," Kate says, reaching for the whiskey bottle. She's only had one shot so far. Looks like we are gearing up for another. "That I could have murdered Alice Walsh."

"You know them better than I do," I say carefully. "What do you think?"

She pours both us another, then she wraps one hand around the sole of her bare foot. She takes a sip. Considers.

"Well," she finally says. "I expect some of them do."

And then all she does is clutch her shot glass and say nothing.

"We could do something about that, too, you know," I say, trying to find a way to comfort her.

"Do what?" she asks, still staring off into the distance.

"We can make some enquiries of our own. See if we can help produce another suspect."

Kate glances at me. Then she looks away again. Puts her fingers to her lips.

"There may be something…"

She hesitates.

"Yes?" I ask.

"There may be something that could help us. Something I haven't told you."

"What? Why?"

"There is a secret I have to keep," she says. "Because I promised that I would. I promised."

"Is this in any way connected with the bloody clothes of Alice's?"

"Yes," she replies, after a moment's hesitation, looking back at me. "With the procedure that she'd had, and why she came to me."

"I want to help," I say. "If you think it helps, tell me."

Kate tilts her head. "I could go and ask her for permission."

"Go where?" I ask, a little confused.

"To the graveyard. To her memorial."

"That's a terrible idea," I say. "Did you hear what Sean said?"

"He'll be gone by now," she says. "They all will."

She reaches for her breast pocket. Realises once more that she no longer has any cigarettes there. "Fuck everything. I'm going."

She is already on her feet. I follow her, hurrying to keep up. "Let me at least put on some shoes before you chase me out into the snow," I begin, but she interrupts me. "No, you're not coming."

I look up at her. "Trust me, I am."

"I'm serious," Kate says, barring my way.

"So am I," I say, incredulous. "Kate, what is the matter?"

She stands firm. "You can't be there. I have to be on my own when I ask her."

"I can sit in the car," I offer, as gently as I can.

"I don't need you sitting in the car!" Kate says fiercely. "I need to be alone. Just for five fucking minutes!"

Breathing hard, she stares at me. Then she adds: "Please."

"Okay," is all I can say. Even as I glance at the letters on the table.

"Good," Kate says back.

She isn't looking at the letters at all.

16:25

I watch her drive off.

For a moment, I consider following her.

Then I go back inside.

It is dark and it is late. My feet are bare and cold on the sitting room floor. My head feels heavy against the sofa. The house and the trees and the wind are making all kinds of noises. You can hear it when you take the time to listen. When you are alone on a sofa in a house that sits all alone on the slopes of the Mountains of Mourne. That is when you hear it. The whisper of sharp branches. Scratching across thin glass and frail stone. Bending in the wind to slap against the wood of the back door. Slap. Slap. Slap.

Scratch. Scratch. Scratch.

The noise of snow falling, silently, soundlessly, as softly as a caress of fingers along your throat.

And then you start imagining that it might not be branches and wind and snow at all.

It might be footsteps.

It might be footsteps at the back of the house. Footsteps wandering down the dark mountains and through the trees. Coming closer and closer. It might be footsteps coming towards the house. Circling it. Working their way towards the back door.

I open my eyes. Shake my head. I should not have had that second glass of whiskey. My vision is a little blurry. I tilt my head to one side, then to the other. Then I try to say "bouillabaisse".

It comes out all right, I suppose.

I sit up and rub my hands across my face. Whenever I

close my eyes, what I see in front of me is the face of Father Daniel, and that will not do.

I haven't even told Kate yet. That I'm into men. Jesus Christ.

I stand up. I need to do something. Walk around. Clear my head. Alcohol is not good for me. It makes me emotional at first, then aggressive. My only excuse is that it's a family trait. My sister suffers from the same condition. Once, we were both walking home drunk and she threw a full paper cup of Coke at a car that was going too fast. The fucker was doing fifty kilometres an hour in a residential zone, it should be said. I almost got beaten up for her pains, but someone must have talked the driver down. Not me, let me tell you. I was ready. Even though I would have almost certainly lost.

I keep walking through the dark house, out into the hall and around the back and into the kitchen. I have not turned on the lights since night fell. I lean against the kitchen sink in the dark, put away the tumbler, then I leave the room. I should get ready for bed.

It is in the hall that I hear it again.

Those noises.

Trees reaching. Branches scratching. Snow softly suffocating.

Footsteps.

Footsteps around the back of the house. Footsteps at the front.

I realise, a little too late, that I might not be imagining them after all. I realise, a little too late, that there is a murderer on the loose.

There is the wind in the trees and the branches scratching against the windows behind the curtains and the soft, soft fall of snow.

And then, there is a clacking noise.

It only takes me a moment to realise that it was the letter box.

I rush out into the hall. There is another slip of paper on the floor.

I bend down to pick up the letter. I read it.

It is in my power to do you harm.

I drop the letter where I stand and throw open the door. Cursing, I stumble out into the darkness. The cold hits me like a baseball bat. My feet are bare, the snow is freezing. It is so dark, too dark, I cannot see anything…

Or was that a movement? Towards the woods?

Before I can check, lights cut through the darkness, bright and blinding. A set of headlights. There is a car coming up the road. As it comes towards me, I recognise the man driving it. It is Daniel.

When he gets out of the driver's seat, I call his name. My feet are cold in the snow. It is as white as Daniel's face.

"Jannis?" he calls out.

"What's the matter?"

He pushes a button. The passenger door opens. He's driving a Tesla. A fucking Tesla.

"Get in," he says. "Kate is in hospital."

Evidence #10564
Notes of the medical examiner (excerpts); victim: Alice Walsh

[...] It is evident that the victim was a healthy young woman prior to death. Her records show that she had undergone no major treatment since early childhood, when she broke an arm. The fracture has healed fully.

So much for the records.

Because it is obvious to this medical professional that she had undergone a procedure very recently. One that was not documented or reported.

It is very likely that the victim aborted a foetus days before her death.

Day 3

FRIDAY 4TH JANUARY 2019

NEIGHBOURHOOD PROTECTION

PROTECT YOUR NEIGHBOURHOOD
*At Neighbourhood Protection we believe in partnership
between the local communities and the police (Policing
and Community Safety Partnerships (PCSPs)). We help
you protect YOURSELF, we help you protect YOUR
property, we help reduce YOUR fear of crime in YOUR
community.*

FIND OUT MORE...
Sean O'Doherty, Rostrevor Rd
Sodsodsod67@hotmail.com

Protect our neighbourhood!
PROTECT OUR WOMEN!!

FIRST MEETING IS HAPPENING!

FEEL SAFE EVERYONE!
WE GOT YOU!
(Bring plenty of water and a rifle/firearm if you got one.
Snacks will be provided. –SOD)

Midnight is a dreadful time to be in a hospital.

Daniel made sure we could still go in. Apparently, he knows the hospital minister. Now we are sitting on two uncomfortable chairs in an empty corridor. Kate is still being examined. She sustained a head wound, probably from a blunt object to the back of her head. The blow was not very powerful, the tired doctor told us, just from a preliminary inspection, but she insisted on running further tests.

Kate was on her way into the examination room when we got to the hospital. The nurse told us to wait. So here we are, two strange men sitting on orange plastic chairs in a windowless corridor, waiting for news. It is too quiet, and the smell of disinfectant is too intense, and everyone is far too tired to be up still.

Daniel has his eyes closed.

"Does it help?" I ask. "Praying?"

He opens his eyes to look at me. They are very clear. "I was not praying," he says, his Scottish accent more pronounced when he is tired, his voice scratchy. "I was thinking about running over the man who did this to her with my car."

"Oh," I say, a little taken aback. "What would God have to say about that?"

"I am not actually going to do it," Daniel says. "That is what matters."

"Is it?" I ask, looking at my hands, carefully folded,

fingers growing older, more wrinkly, thicker. "Does it not matter what we want, or what we imagine we might do?"

From the corner of my eye, I see that Daniel is not looking away from me. "It matters if you want it to."

"I was raised a Catholic," I explain. "In the confessional, it was all about what we thought and what we wanted. It was only rarely ever about what we had done."

"Was it because you never did anything wrong?" Daniel asks gently. "Was it because you always stopped yourself in time?"

I shrug. Search for a topic of conversation that is safer. "I didn't picture you to be the sort to be driving a Tesla."

"Ah."

The sound he makes is a little embarrassed and a little gleeful. I look over to see that he has leaned back, dropping his head against the wall, laughing silently. The line of his throat is long. "It was a gift. It's completely inappropriate, of course, not to mention that I basically have to cross the border to find a supercharger, but I just didn't know how to say no. I mean, if somebody offers you something like that, how do you turn them down? It belonged to an elderly lady in the congregation, she couldn't use it anymore…"

"Ah, that's it then?" I tease. "You accepted it in the name of charity? Being a good Christian?"

"Bugger off!," he says, laughing still, though no longer silently.

I raise both hands in mock defence.

"No, you're right, it's a great car," he goes on, almost unprompted. "The acceleration is incredible, remind me to show you on the way back, there's a stretch of road where no one ever goes, it's perfectly safe…"

He peters out. Suddenly, I have to look away from him. Distance myself. Remind myself why we are here. Who we are waiting for to wake up. "So you think it was a man, then? Who did this to her?" I ask.

"I was wondering whether it was the same person," Daniel replies.

"The same person?"

"Kate's attacker and Alice's murderer."

"Then you don't think it was her?"

"Of course I don't," Dan says. "You'd have to be mad to think that. Kate couldn't hurt a fly."

"Well, someone does. They're sending her threatening letters, after all."

Daniel sits forward so suddenly it almost makes me recoil. "What?"

"Kate received a threatening letter after she was released by the police," I explain. "And another letter was delivered tonight."

Daniel looks away. Then he looks down.

"She didn't tell you, I take it," I say.

"She told you, though," he says, looking back up at me. Is it hostility I see in his expression? Jealousy? Disappointment?

"Well, I was the one who found the first letter," I say. "So it couldn't really be avoided."

He says nothing to that.

Instead, he leans across to me after ten minutes of silence. "Are you saying you knew that she'd received threatening letters, but you still let her go to the graveyard all on her own?"

Now it is up to me not to say anything.

It is half an hour later that the doctor releases Kate into our care. I want to ask her if she remembers anything the first chance I get, but Daniel takes one look at her face, puts an arm around her shoulders and says: "Let's get you home."

The car is moving through the darkness in almost perfect silence, the roads empty, white snow reflecting the cold headlights.

"Who found me?" Kate asks, making a valiant attempt to sound as if it cost her nothing to say the words. Her head is bandaged.

"Me," Daniel answers, eyes fixed on the road. He is well beyond the speed limit and does not seem about to slow down. Another rage driver. Make no mistake, I will be behind the steering wheel from now on. Between the two of them, they might get us killed.

Kate glances at him. "Did you want to check on Alice?" she asks quietly.

I look at him then, too. Because it's quite convenient, isn't it?

That he arrived just at the right time. Just the right place. Almost as if he knew where to be.

"It was very lucky you were there," I ask. "The attacker couldn't have been gone for long. Did you see anyone?"

Daniel shakes his head. "The only person I saw was you. Your body on the ground, Kate."

But he isn't looking at either of us. He is staring, staring, staring, straight ahead, at nothing but the road.

I cannot help but keep glancing at Father Daniel as he drives us home.

Once we arrive at Kate's, Daniel insists on accompanying us inside. I watch him closely. I promise myself I will not let Kate be alone from now on, not with him nor anyone else.

I stand in the kitchen, preparing tea, shamelessly eavesdropping on the conversation Daniel and Kate are having down the hall, in front of the bedroom.

"It's all right," Kate says. "All I want is to go to sleep, really."

A pause. Then Daniel speaks again: "You sure you don't want me to stay?"

I am sure it is meant to come out kindly, but instead he sounds tense.

"Where would you sleep?" she asks, almost laughing.

"Erm," he says. "The bed."

"Then where would we put Jannis?"

Another pause. This one longer than the last. "He's sleeping in there with you, then?"

"You know what the guest room looks like. I wasn't going to make him sleep among the paint buckets, Dan."

"How kind of you."

The irony in his voice could not be more obvious. Neither could the annoyance in Kate's: "Don't be like that."

"Concerned?" he asks, sharply.

But not as sharply as her: "Jealous."

Daniel seems to consider his answer carefully. Then he says: "You're shutting me out."

I can almost see Kate throw up her arms: "Jan and I have slept in the same bed for nineteen years. Get over it."

"No, I mean, you're shutting me out of this," he says. "You didn't tell me about the threats."

This time, it is Kate who draws out the silence. I remember the list on the coffee table. Daniel's name on it. "I wanted to," she says. "When I came to the church today."

"You could have texted," he says.

Silence.

"I'll call you tomorrow," he tells her, just as she says, "Let's talk tomorrow, okay?"

Quiet laughter. A chuckle. The chuckle is hers, I recognise it, so the laughter must be his. I wonder if he looks like he did in the hospital corridor, head thrown back and grinning widely.

On his way out, Daniel stops in the kitchen. Standing in the doorframe, he waves goodbye. His fingers are long and thin. "Good night."

"Good night, Father," I say.

That gives him pause. He looks at me. Then he turns away without another word. I do not hear him drive off. All I see are the headlights cutting across the mountain slopes and then down the road and out of sight.

I take the tea into the bedroom. Kate is already in her pyjamas, sitting on the bed. I hand her the tea, then I take the letter I found this evening out of my pocket and put it down on the bedspread.

She picks it up gingerly.

"It was dropped off just before Daniel got here," I explain. "I did not see anyone, though."

Kate runs a finger along the edges of the piece of paper, reading the words threatening her with physical harm. "Seems like they acted first and warned me later, doesn't it?" Her brow furrows. "Is that a Bible quote, do you think?"

It is difficult to look at her face, so I look at her hands instead. "Daniel thinks it was Alice Walsh's murderer who attacked you."

Her voice is tense when she speaks next. "And you think it was Daniel."

I sigh. I am careful not to look at her still. "I'd rather not. But it's very convenient, don't you think?"

"That he saved my life?" she asks, the challenge in her voice obvious.

It raises my hackles. I'm not the enemy here. "No, that he was there just in time."

"I was lucky," she says stubbornly. "He is the priest. It is his graveyard. Why aren't you looking at me?"

I look up. Into her thin, determined face.

"If I had come with you, this would not have happened," I say, quite miserably.

"You're being stupid," she insists. "This isn't your fault. It's the fault of the person who hit me over the head."

But there is a tremor to her voice. She does not want me to know that she is scared, but she is.

"The violence is escalating," I say quietly. "We should do something."

Kate nods, her expression turning grim. "Yes, we should."

I nod, too. We begin speaking at the same time:

"We need to find out who is sending these letters…," I say.

"We need to find Alice Walsh's killer," she says.

We stare at each for a moment. "You with me?" she asks, and it isn't well above a whisper.

"I'm always with you," I say promptly.

"Good," she says. "Then there's something I need to tell you. The secret. About the procedure."

"I have nowhere to be," I say.

Kate nods. She reaches for the pillow. She hugs it to her chest.

And then she tells me.

I stare at Kate once she has finished.

So Alice Walsh had an abortion. That was the procedure she went through. One week before she was gruesomely murdered, she has an abortion, taking two pills that she ordered on the Internet, after asking Kate about them. Alice Walsh swallows them. The same night, she wakes up, bleeding profusely. She makes it all the way to Kate's house and rings the doorbell. Kate helps her in and takes care of her. That's how Kate got stuck with her bloody clothes, because Alice Walsh did not want her parents to find out. That was why Kate came around for a house call on the day of Alice's death, when her parents were not in.

"She made me swear not to tell anyone," Kate says. "I told the police, of course, but I don't think that anybody else knows." Her fingers are drawing erratic patterns onto the bed sheets. I swallow, watching Kate's fingers.

"Who was the father?" I ask Kate.

She just shakes her head. "She wouldn't say."

"Fuck," I curse. "*Verdammte Scheiße.*" Because it feels so much better to swear in German sometimes.

"But I've been thinking," Kate adds, worrying her lip. "You know the way Alice's body was positioned? With her body parts... puzzled back together?"

I stare at her. Horror is already sweeping through me as she goes on: "There is this myth that, after an abortion, you have to find all the body parts of the foetus and put it back together, like a puzzle, to make sure you didn't miss

113

anything. Obviously that's not true, but it is persistent. That's what Alice's body reminded me of."

We turn off the lights eventually, but I cannot go to sleep.

If only Alice Walsh had told Kate who the father was. A woman scorned, the saying goes, but try telling a man you have taken something away from him that he considers his own. Depending on the man, this might get you into very real trouble, or so my sister says. She should know, being a detective.

Next to me, Kate shifts in her sleep. Then she turns onto her other side, facing me. I look at the line of her face, the tufts of her hair, anything I can see in the darkness. The white fabric of the bandage, for one.

She may pretend that she is not frightened, but know her well. I do not want to see her frightened. And I promise myself that I will protect her. No matter the cost.

Another morning spent at the police station in Newry. I insisted we file charges. I also insisted that I drive. Kate agreed, thank God.

Of course, I know that the police are up to their neck in the murder investigation. Kate discovered the body on Tuesday, I flew in on Wednesday, today is Friday, and they have not made any more arrests. Detective Inspector Adam Kwiatkowski looks harrowed.

It is still morning by the time we are on our way back. Kate is wringing her hands. I wonder if she even realises. "I have to open the practice today. This sitting around, it isn't helping. My patients need me. GPs are far and few between in rural Ireland."

I nod. It will do her good to be back at work.

"You're right," I say. "They need you."

Rostrevor Road is as windswept as ever. I dropped off Kate at her practice, then set off for her house. Clouds are collecting in the sky, heavy and grey, as if it is about to rain, when I drive past Megan Walsh's home.

There is a group of men standing in front of it. Two of them are waving at me, motioning for me to pull over. I recognise Sean O'Doherty and William O'Rawe and turn into the driveway. Sean is smoking, so is William. The group seem mostly to be standing around.

When I have come to a stop, Sean flips away his cigarette and comes towards me. William O'Rawe follows suit, also getting rid of his cigarette.

Sean plants his feet and knocks against my window. He is wearing a smile.

"License and registration," he says. He laughs. I laugh with him, although I most decidedly do not feel like laughing. "Is anything the matter?" I ask.

"No, just having a bit of a meeting," he says. "We set up the Neighbourhood Protection, under the PCSP, O'Rawe and me. I'm the co-ordinator."

"A little chilly, having a meeting out here," I point out.

"We just want Meg and Pat to feel safe," Sean says.

He points towards the front of the house.

I swallow.

Rifles. Arranged in a neat row, ordered by size. Standing upright against the white wood. Hunting weapons, as far as I can tell. I count six.

"Whose are those?" I ask.

"Not to worry," Sean replies, clapping me on the shoulder "All with the proper permits, of course."

"Of course," I say, doing my very best to ignore the uncomfortable sensation settling at the pit of my stomach. "Well, if you don't mind, I'll be on my—"

"Kate not with you, then?"

"No," I say. "She's at work."

"At work, is she?" Sean spits on the ground. "Fancy that."

"Where else would she be?"

"Oh, nowhere. Just makes me laugh, that she'd go to work."

"Why?" I ask.

Sean grins.

Before he has time to say anything else, the front door of the house is opened. Megan Walsh steps out. "Is it her?" she calls out.

Sean straightens. "No, just her fuckboy."

"If you don't mind," I say, "I really must be going."

But Megan Walsh is already calling out: "Ask him in, will you, Sean?"

Then she turns around and walks back inside.

I stare at her. Then I stare at Sean.

He shrugs. "Looks like you're getting out, mate."

He doesn't seem to be asking.

I get out of the car and lock it. Then I walk up to the house and enter.

Megan Walsh has already gone on ahead, through the hall, past a set of stairs and into the kitchen. I follow her.

She puts the kettle on as I stand at the kitchen island. It is state-of-the-art, outfitted with all the latest equipment, a massive fridge with an ice dispenser, a steamer and a regular as well as a pizza oven.

She glances at me as she takes out the tea bags. "You a Catholic?" she asks me gruffly.

Taken aback, I can do nothing but nod, although I haven't practised my faith in years.

"Well, that at least." She takes out the teabags.

She puts two cups and saucers on the kitchen island. They are very fine and match the teapot she takes out next. She bends down to take a matching sugar bowl out of the cupboard. She puts it down with a huff, then turns to the kettle. "The detectives aren't. The one in charge of this case. He's a Protestant." The kettle begins to emit a shrill whistle. "They don't care about us. It's always been the powerful helping the powerful in this country, and we've always been second-class citizens."

"I would like to think that the police will do their best to bring Alice justice," I say, in the hopes of offering some comfort.

"And what good is that going to do?"

Megan's hand is wrapped around the handle of the kettle. She turns around to look at me. Straight at me. Her voice is suddenly so harsh, as hot and boiling as the water. She pours it into the teapot, but it is going everywhere. Running down the side of the pot. Splashing onto the kitchen island. "What good is justice going to do my daughter? She'll still be dead."

I get a kitchen towel from the roll hanging on a small

fashionable rack next to her. "You don't have to," she says, eyes closed for a moment, looking guilty and stubborn at the same time, stubbornly determined not to fall apart.

I almost press her arm. Almost give her an embrace.

Then all I do is wipe up the water. "Is your husband here?" I ask gently.

Megan huffs again. "He has been going for walks. That's what he says, anyway. Walking to Will's house, most likely, and shooting at tin cans with his old mucker." She rubs her hands across her cheeks, once, twice, like a woman pinching her own cheeks to make it look as if she is wearing rouge. "In and out at all hours. This morning, last night, no time's too odd for him. He doesn't care what everyone will think. What I'll think."

"And you?" I ask, concerned. "You just stay in here, all on your own, when he is gone? You were all alone last night?"

For a moment, I see it flash across her face. An expression that makes me think that my questions scare her.

"I am worried for you," I say, I clarify.

Megan's mouth twists. She pours us tea. "I'm not. I was alone last night, and I'm not worried."

"Is there anything I can do for you?" I ask, taking the saucer from her grip.

Her fingers are freezing cold.

"Yes," she says. She lifts her own cup to her lips. Takes a sip. Closes her eyes. "You can tell your friend to leave."

"Excuse me?"

Megan Walsh opens her eyes. Some of her lipstick now sits on the white porcelain of the cup. Her cold hands, and the red lipstick looks like a wound in her face, her dark eyes like bruises blooming. "Pack up. Move away. Plenty of places to live. She isn't welcome here anymore."

"Mrs Walsh, I want you to believe me when I tell you that Kate had nothing to do with your daughter's death."

"And how would you know?" Megan Walsh asks. "You weren't here. You don't know what Alice was like, this last year. She was gone so much. Since last summer, she spent so much time out of the house. And then this Christmas, she was barely there. Even when she was here, she seemed a million miles away. Spent all her time with those twins."

"Which twins, Mrs Walsh? Are they friends from school?"

Megan Walsh shakes her head. "My daughter wasn't popular at school."

"But there were some classmates of hers at the vigil…"

"Everyone comes to the bloody vigil," Megan Walsh hisses. "For them, it's a show, isn't it? It's dramatic. They can be dramatic there. But in school, they picked on my daughter. No, it isn't them that Alice spent her time with. It's the twins from the South. Betha and Enda. The last days of her life, and she spent them with two people who are as good as strangers."

She is not crying. But she looks as if she might. "I will pass on your message, Mrs Walsh," I say as I rise. "But you could not have known. There was nothing you could have done."

She laughs. It is such a painful sound. Like a hooligan kicking your face in. "Did you know," she says. "I did not want Alice."

I stare at her.

"I was on my way to England already to have her removed. I was already at the airport." She swipes her thumb across the lipstick stain on the porcelain, staring off into the distance, smearing the colour. "Seventeen years ago."

She bites her lip. Red stains on her teeth. "Pregnant at forty-one. Who could have expected that? Who could have wanted that? I would have boarded the plane if Pat hadn't dragged me back. And since then, my very first thought waking up in the morning, for seventeen years, was for her. My very last, going to sleep at night, was for her. Because I love her so much. I never thought I would. The wee dote I almost murdered, and I loved her so much. We were best friends."

She looks back at me. "Every morning. Every night. There was no me. There was only her."

Eyes like bruises, boring into me. "That's why you better make sure you get the message across loud and clear, Mr Loose. She better get out of here. She isn't welcome here anymore."

I go. I even pretend that I do not see how her shoulders begin to shake with the tears she can no longer hold back.

As I drive off, I look at the rifles, leaning against the wall.

I go find Kate at her practice. I want to have an eye on her, after all, and she can possibly help with those mysterious twins.

Her receptionist is there.

The waiting room is empty.

Entirely empty.

"I thought there were appointments?" I ask Kate, the moment the receptionist has shown me through.

"Yes," she says, dressed in her white lab coat and scrubs, all the tools of her trade spread out, yearning to be used. "So far, no one's showed up, so it is."

I did not have the heart to ask her any questions as we sat and waited in her practice. Waited all day.

No one came by. All the appointments were cancelled; patients, when called at home, said they had forgotten and they did not want to make a new one, either.

No one.

So we went home. I made dinner, vegetarian lasagne, while Kate showered and changed. And then we had it. And a stiff drink. And now I am filling the dishwasher in the kitchen.

Kate is leaning against the kitchen sink, arms crossed, wearing a chequered silk blouse and her lime-green Paul Smith, a suit she has had for years, bought when it still cost her an entire month's wages. This is the suit she wears when she needs her clothes to hold her together. Her right foot is crossed behind her ankle. She is the picture of poise. I know that this isn't a good sign. "So, while I was sitting there waiting for someone to show up, I had a look online. I thought, I don't know. I thought maybe there was a killer who'd done something like this before. Cut up the body like that."

"Right."

"There isn't," she says. "No record online of any other psycho killers running around cutting people up and putting their limbs back together. Apparently, in all the other cases, limbs were taken away and kept as trophies." She shifts. "Although there was this one case thirty years back, here in Mountains, too, where the murderer treated his victim in a similar manner, after she'd had a miscarriage; he was tried and got a fairly lenient sentence. The judge was very much on his side. A woman judge, by the way. Oh, and the papers also seemed to think it wasn't all that bad what he'd done."

I prick my ears. Kate's expression darkens even further. "Don't get overly excited. It's a dead end. The murderer has been dead for six years. The judge is retired now, too."

I close the dishwasher and go to lean up against the kitchen cupboards across from her, my own arms crossed, the pine-coloured sweater soft against my fingers. "Your patients will be back," I say gently.

She looks to the side. Her face is framed by the window leading out onto the drive and the slopes of the mountains. The moon is shining. The snow reflects its light, turning the night into a pale thing. It is like twilight out, only darker. Stranger.

I take a sip from the mug I am holding. "Megan Walsh asked me in today when I drove past her house."

"What? Why?"

"Asked me to tell you to pack up and move away."

Kate looks at the floor. "Fuck," she says.

"She also told me that her daughter had not been spending much time at home since the previous summer. And almost all of her Christmas holidays with two friends."

"From school?"

"No. Apparently, Alice Walsh was picked on in school. Did you know?"

Kate shakes her head, but her expression is growing grimmer and grimmer.

"Who are the twins?"

Kate's brow furrows. Then her expression smooths over. "Must be Betha and Enda. They're from the South. They were the two young people in the front pew at the vigil. I believe they were visiting Alice Walsh for the holidays. From Cork, I think, they are. Or that's where they met. Alice spent a couple of weeks there in the summer. They met on the beach, or something? Aye, aye, they did. They're staying at a guest house in Killowen, right by the sea, fifteen minutes down the road. Said they'd come for Kilbroney Park. It think I saw them a few times, having cake at the Church Café in Rostrevor. It's lovely, that café. Not a church anymore. Anyway, the guesthouse is part of another bit of Elizabeth Adams's property, I think, William's managing it for her."

"Maybe we should talk to them?" I suggest. "Teenagers are usually more willing to trust someone their age. They might know something about the pregnancy."

Kate nods, then goes back to staring into her mug. "I had a visitor while you were gone," she finally says. "It was Florence. Florence O'Rawe."

"What did she want?"

Kate jerks her head at the oven. A casserole sits on top of it, covered in tin foil. "She made stew. Thought I would need it, what with the head injury."

"How kind of her," I say. "Did she also bring some paracetamol?"

"You should have seen her," she says, her face drawn.

"She parked the car down the road, in that lay-over, you know? I've never had anyone be so eager not to be seen with me."

"At least she did not hit you over the head, or drop off threatening letters, or ask you to move away," I point out.

"There's that," Kate says and clinks her mug against mine. She takes a sip, then looks back at me. "Just, something occurred me while she was standing there, putting the casserole in the oven."

"And what was that?"

Kate swallows visibly. "How did she know I'd been injured?"

"Grapevine?" I suggest. "Small community?"

"Did you tell anyone?" Kate asks.

"No. Daniel?"

"I called him," she says. "To ask him if he'd told anyone. And guess what? He said no."

"He might be lying," I point out.

"What is it with you and Daniel?" she asks, frowning. "He's a jealous prick, fine, but what's your problem?"

I look at her. Her face, framed by the window looking out into the night. The still grey night.

I can feel my adrenaline spike before my brain has even registered what I am seeing.

The night is not still.

Something is moving on the other side of the window.

"Kate," I hiss, "get away from the window!"

She stumbles across the kitchen to join me. I hit the light switch next to me, throwing us into darkness.

There are the trees, the cowering rowans and tall pines,

128

swaying silently in the wind and the weight of the snow. The mountains stretch out beyond the road, white and ghostly as fog in the light of the moon.

Maybe it was only the trees. Their branches moving in the wind. The rowan and their branches, scratching against the kitchen window. The light of the moon, falling as silently as snow.

Then I spot another movement.

There is someone standing out there. A dark silhouette, stark and clear against the snow.

They are holding a rifle.

There they are. Standing outside. Holding the rifle.

Waiting.

Watching.

They seem to be looking at us.

"Can you tell who it is?" I ask.

She stares. And stares. "No," she says under her breath. "No, it's too dark."

"Call the police," I say, not letting the silhouette out of my sight, "right now!"

She does.

I watch the silhouette. My blood is pounding in my ears. There is nothing I can do against a rifle. The blood keeps pounding. The adrenaline is rising. Nothing I can do. Stay still. Wait for the police.

That is what they want, I realise, and it makes my blood roar. They want us to cower. They want us afraid.

It takes the police thirty minutes to get here. The moment their sirens can be heard, the silhouette slips away into the trees.

They are leaving. Not down the road.

Into the woods.

The Detective Constables try to be helpful, but it's dark and we cannot even prove anyone was there. I thought I saw them leave towards the woods, but when we look for footprints, there is nothing much useful, at least not while it is still dark. We go with them to the station, report the incident.

By the time they drive us back, both Kate and I are dead on our feet.

Still, I find it impossible to go to sleep. Kate is lying next to me, breathing regularly.

I lie awake and listen for any noises. For boots in the snow. The rustle of clothes. The sounds of heavy cold breath, fogging up the window, because they are standing right in front of the glass. Because they are watching us.

I sit up so suddenly. My blood is thrumming. "Kate," I say, shaking her shoulder. I am trying to go for gentle, but my grip is stronger than I want it to be. "Switch sides with me."

She mumbles something, her face crunching up. "'y?"

"You should not be next to the window."

"… being stupid…"

She tries to turn away from me, but I keep holding onto her shoulder. "Come on," I say, pulling her back towards me, and I am shocked to hear that it does not sound like a plea. It sounds like an order.

For a moment, our eyes meet. She is looking at me in a strange way. She is so still. Looking so closely.

I can't bear that expression on her face right now. I do not know what it means. All I need is for her to be out of harm's way. I pull at her once more. She allows me to cajole her onto my side of the bed before turning back onto her side, away from me.

I close my eyes. There is sweat on my brow. Sweat on my skin, from my neck down to the back of my knees. I try and match my breathing to Kate's. It will calm me down.

The blood still pumping, pumping, pumping. I feel so impotent. So helpless.

I do not know how much time has passed when I hear the noise. Scraping. Crunching.

Are those steps?

My palms are sweaty when I glance out through the blinds.

My blood freezes.

There they are. Walking around the house, trailing the rifle behind them. The silhouette is too far away for me to recognise them. They are keeping close to the trees. Walking slowly.

And then the head turns.

They are looking straight at me.

I let the blinds fall shut. The fear is overwhelming. There is nowhere to go, nowhere to run, you have to wait, wait for them to come to you, and they are. Step by step, they are coming.

I get up. I am not going to fucking cower. I walk out into the hall, past the back door to get into the sitting room.

Only I do not make it quite that far.

When I walk through the corridor, I realise that there is a new letter. This time, it has been pushed through the slit under the back door.

I go get a scarf, wrap it around my hand, then pick it up.

Do not fret because of those who are evil or be envious of those who do wrong; for like the grass they will soon wither, like green plants they will soon die away.

My fingers are cold again. I push open the back door, my blood hot, my fists shaking. I am not thinking. I am charging. Charging out of the door and into the white night.

But there is no one there anymore.

There is no sign of the silhouette.

No sign of a rifle.

There is nothing.

NOTES
DETECTIVE CONSTABLE NORAH BAILEY INTERVIEWING
(FOLLOW-UP TO DOOR-TO-DOOR)
ELIZABETH ADAMS
3 MAIN STREET
BT34 4DDX

But of course. Please, come in. Of course we can have a chat. You know me. I do like a chat. No, I quite enjoyed our conversation last time. I could not believe it when you told me about the bloody clothes.

Oh, I know you shouldn't have done that. But not to worry. I am sure no harm was done.

No, I do not mind at all if you sit. It must be tiring, this work that you do. Forgive the boots. I was just outside in the garden. The poplar mushroom season has started, as you know, and I was hoping to find a few early specimens. I was down by the trees, they prefer black poplar trees and willows, you know. My father planted the black poplars specifically in the hopes that the mushrooms would choose them as their habitat. And for the sake of the trees themselves, of course. Did you know that they are the most endangered tree in England? They are almost extinct in the wild now, and grow mostly in parks and gardens and by riversides, especially in Cumbria, where I was born. They are tall and bushy, beautiful trees, with a thick bark. Sturdy, steady, like the country itself. And do you know about the yew trees? England counts the highest number of yew trees in the world. Some of them are ancient. Two thousand, perhaps even five thousand years old. And they enjoy no protection from the law at all. Anyone can cut them down when they are on private property.

You have never seen a yew tree? But of course you have. There is one in the churchyard. And then there is one on Kate O'Leary's property. She has thought about cutting it down, did you know that? It is a disgrace. She has been on this Earth for forty years, and she has the nerve to decide that she is entitled to cut down a tree that may be thousands of years old. All of that land once used to belong to my family. There were so many more trees back then, the black poplar with their burls, growing around infections like shields, defending the aging tree, and the yews with their limbs as thick and sturdy as a castle wall.

Yes, I have been reading a lot of nature writing. And I will still be wanting back my copy of *A Month in the Country*, if you please. Don't pretend both of us don't know who has checked it out of the library cart and has not returned it yet. I donated it to the cart, and I would appreciate seeing it back there.

But you must be here about poor Alice Walsh. How did I hear? Oh, love, how did anybody hear? It is a little hard to miss, isn't it, when the police drive through the town with their sirens blaring? Don't you know that this was the first time, the first time I can ever remember the police having used the siren in Annacairn? Not even during the Troubles. In Newry, yes, with all the British troop transports coming from the coast. I remember that there was an explosion once, and William outside playing football, and he and his friends turned just one corner and saw the burnt-out army vehicle and the dead bodies of the soldiers. That was when I knew this was not where we would be living. No, there were no sirens in Annacairn. Unless my memory tricks me. It feels far away, does it not? Well, to you, it must have. Were you even alive for them? I am sure you weren't. Just like Alice Walsh. You have known nothing but peace.

It feels like history to you, you say? All you learned about in school were Vikings and kings and mediaeval battles? Well, it is different for us. My brother, a Detective Sergeant at the time, he was kidnapped on the border by the IRA in the 1990s. All he had done was go on a fishing trip. They tortured him for five days before they summarily executed him. All we got back was his body in parts.

So, yes, I heard the sirens. I was out in the garden, checking for mushrooms. I was paying close attention because they are easy to confuse with other fieldcap mushrooms. William and Tessa were with me, good enough to help their mother out in the garden. They had spent the night. William and Tessa do not see eye to eye, of course. William can be a bit of a fool sometimes. He married a Republican, for one.

You thought my son and I were not on visiting terms? Oh, no, you would be quite wrong. I love my son. I would do anything for him. And so would his sister. We are family. An old family. My family has owned land here even before the Irish Rebellion. That was in 1641. My forefathers were part of the Protestant Ascendancy. Of course, this is all long ago. But old roots do not wither. They reach deep. They are stronger than you think.

Oh, yes, it is true. Catholics could not vote or attend the Irish Parliament back then. You may consider that unjust. Look at you, I can see your expression turning all dark. But these days, I feel like my voice barely counts anymore at all. Simply because I am old. Take the referendum; ask for the will of the people, but when you do not like the will of the people, you say that it is too many of the elderly voting, and that is the only reason why Leave won. As if we weren't part of the people simply because we are old. As if we did not matter anymore. As if it wasn't bad enough that I had to give up my wonderful car. All electric, too. Not too old to know what is good for the planet, I assure you!

It does feel very much like that. As if the elderly did not matter anymore. I hardly recognise the country I live in these days. I used to be a judge, as I am sure you are aware. When I practised the law, it ensured order. Now, all the law seems to do is let people get off with slaps on the wrist. The moment they legalise abortion, you might as well abolish all courts. Just let everyone walk around murdering and pillaging, why don't we?

But I am boring you, aren't I? You young people believe this is all a little sectarian, don't you? Alice certainly thought so. She was so young but had such strong opinions already.

God, Norah, isn't it terrible? Or should I call you Detective Constable when you are on duty? Of course, I can do that. It feels odd only because I have known you ever since you were a little girl, coming to get all your reading material from the library cart. Most of those books were donations from my library.

No, you are right. This isn't what you have come here to talk about. But I simply do not know what to say. It was William who told me that Alice Walsh was dead. That they had found her body, and that you had taken in Kate for questioning. Nothing came of it, I suppose, since you released her? It is frightening, is it not, to think that a doctor would be involved in such a crime? To think of how many times I sat in her office, looking at that scalpel on her desk, a touching, if ludicrous gift of her parents'. Then again, from my time as a judge, I know it is silly to think of doctors as better people. They commit crimes just the same as any other profession. And their crimes tend to have more dire consequences.

There is that man visiting her. Jannis Loose, his name is, I believe. Like Janice Joplin. From Germany. Not a Nazi, of course. At least not as far as I can tell.

No, no, he is all right. Quite all right. I will say, I do not see why he should involve himself so much. It is hardly any of his business, all of this, is it? But I am glad someone is taking care of Kate. She must be frightened out of her wits, with the threats she has been receiving. You are aware of those, aren't you? Are you doing anything about that?

Had I noticed anything unusual about Alice Walsh? Well, let me think. I did not see much of her, of course, except for when she helped me out with my library. It needs sorting out. Before I leave this mortal coil.

Anything unusual…

Well, I don't know.

It does not seem decent.

I trust that this will remain confidential.

If it goes to court, of course, but until then…

Alice went to Cork for her summer holiday. And I thought she came back changed. She seemed more secretive. Maybe even a little angry. Confused. And she seemed to have trouble in school. The other girls were teasing her.

No, I could not possibly tell you what about.

I would have no clue whatsoever.

Except that there was perhaps a hint in the books she chose to steal from my library.

Oh yes. She stole my classics. She took them without telling me and never returned them. My copy of *The Well of Loneliness*. *Nana*, by Emile Zola, I am sure you have heard of it. *Q. E. D.* by Gertrude Stein. And *Mrs Dalloway*, by our very own Virginia Woolf.

You do not know what these books have in common?

They are about love affairs between women, Detective Constable.

Make of that what you will. I know nothing for certain. But perhaps Father Daniel does?

What do you mean, Alice Walsh never went to church? Of course she did.

Oh no, not to mass. She went in secret. To confession, perhaps?

I am sure there is a harmless explanation why she went in secret. Maybe she did not want her parents to know, or her mother at least, who had been so adamant Alice practise the faith. Perhaps Alice did not want her mother to know that she had finally succeeded in her cajoling, her threats, her pleas.

Or perhaps there was another reason. But why would you keep church visits secret? What reason could there be?

How do I know? From Tessa. Tessa cleans the church, on Tuesdays and Thursdays, when there is no mass. Did you not know that?

Alice Walsh was there. Every Tuesday. Every Thursday. As if there was something weighing on her conscience. She always met with Father Daniel. Always just the two of them. She might have confided in him, mightn't she?

Why did I not say so the first time you came knocking?

Oh, goodness. I did not think that it was important.

Day 4

SATURDAY 5TH JANUARY 2019

EVIDENCE #10599
CATEGORY: DIARY, VICTIM'S
DESCRIPTION:
DIARY OF ALICE WALSH, DISCONTINUED FOR UNKNOWN
REASONS AFTER THE SUMMER OF 2018

1/8/2018

Still in Cork. Met someone today. Two someones, I guess. Betha and Enda. They're twins. It's funny, twins. They're funny. More than funny. We met on the beach, can you imagine? Because it's been pissing down, that's why it's funny, and that's why it happened in the first place: hard to overlook the only two other nutcases out in that weather. But I like to walk by the sea in the rain. It looks so wild. So wild.

And the sound of raindrops on my hood, that's also beautiful.

They speak Gaelic. And French. I know because they helped a French couple find their way to the public loos, after we'd left the beach. I want to learn Gaelic. It sounds beautiful. It is going to be this huge issue though. Maybe I should learn French instead. That's not going to be as much of an issue, maybe.

I wonder if it's difficult. Learning another language. I never really gave it a serious go in school I think and now school's almost over and Betha and Enda, when they go to uni they'll do semesters abroad in Paris and I'll be stuck in Belfast or Dublin. Fuck everything.

4/8/2018

Every day with Enda and Betha. Enda has to leave tomorrow. He's going to a summer school in Prague at the uni there because he's this fucking over-achiever. It's sad. We got sloshed. It's morning now. Last night was wild though. It was really beautiful.

We talked about learning Gaelic. They said I should. I said it's an issue. They said it shouldn't be an issue, it's a language, languages are there to help you communicate with people. It's awesome when you can suddenly understand people you couldn't understand before.

I laughed. Language is there to be spun, I said, to make you believe shit that isn't true. Like the whole referendum bullshit.

I think I shocked them. Betha especially. I really didn't want to shock her. I want to…

I want to impress her.

6/8/2018

You know what I found out? They'd been raised with Gaelic. They had to learn English in kindergarten. They learned my language, so that they could talk to me. Did I learn their language? No, I didn't. Here the two of them are, making all these plans, going to summer schools in Prague and semesters in Paris, and my universe extended as far as Dublin and maybe Edinburgh or London. I mean, what the fuck? There's a whole world out there and I'm like no I can't learn Gaelic that's too much of an issue. Why is that a fucking issue? Who's decided that it is? And you know maybe I also wanna go to Paris or Prague or whatever, but with Brexit, that isn't going to happen, is it? The future doesn't look so bright anymore, suddenly. And the suicide rates in the North are through the roof. Maybe it's because… I don't know what that is.

I thought maybe it would be awkward with Betha, without Enda, but it's not.

I am so glad.

9/8/2018

She'll come to visit. In the winter. She promised. And Enda will come, too. I wonder if this is for real. Or if we will all realise, once I am back home and we don't get to see each other every day anymore, that we were just friends for a season.

I hope we won't.

Though, maybe.

Maybe it'd be better.

Then I could stop wondering.

Why I feel so drawn to her.

10/8/2018

I'm happy.

God, I am so very happy.

I kissed her.

11/8/2018

Okay, so we were both drunk last night, and it was my last night, and I think that's why we kissed. We were drunk. And I didn't want to go. I wanted to see her again, and not be in a different country from hers. But I'm back home now. Crossed the border. Not that there was anything to cross. But there might be. Soon. And then what? I mean, what the fuck. What the actual fuck. This is one thousand fucking per cent unnecessary. One thousand fucking per cent. One thousand fucking per cent. And it's not like the majority of people here said they wanted out. It's the British bastards, isn't it, that want out? Well, they can fucking go if they fucking want to.

13/8/2018

Told Elizabeth about Betha and Enda today, when I helped her sort through her books. She made a joke, consorting with the enemy. Ha-fucking-ha. Might have snapped at her. Might also have taken a few books.

Not stolen. I'll return them.

I don't know where to keep them. They are all... books about...

Women who love women. Or women who love women and men. Queer women.

Am I queer?

I can't be.

It's just... It's just Betha.

It's just that I miss them. Betha and Enda.

Especially Betha.

Fuck.

What my mum would have to say about that.

I can't be. I can't be.

What if I am?

School would turn into hell. Life would turn into hell. My whole life.

Fuck. Shit.

Maybe if I just slept with a man... Because I haven't. Never before. Not yet.

But maybe if I did, then I'd know. Whether that's for me.

Yes, I need to find someone who'll do it. Someone who won't ever tell my parents.

21/8/2018

I know who. He'd never tell Mum and Dad. And then, when Enda and Betha come to visit, I'll know. I'll know what to do. What to tell Betha. And how.

He's perfect.

It is the bright light of morning, the police have been here and left again, and we are dressed and back at the living-room table, bent over the threatening letters. Kate is wearing a grey chequered suit; she loves suits so much because she came from nothing, and it still makes her feel real when she puts one on. As if she was someone. And she needs to feel like she is someone just now, a real person, not a doctor whose practice is empty.

I am wearing a wool cardigan, anything to warm the cold fear out of my blood. Kate is still looking at the new letter, her brow furrowed, fingers against her lips, leaning over the table. Her fingers are as elegant as her legs, all her limbs made to dance. It physically hurts, imagining what these fingers would look like smashed to mush with the heavy butt of a rifle. These legs, perforated by six, seven, twenty bullets. It hurts even more because we are fighting. About the letter.

"They are Bible quotations," I point out.

"Anyone can pick up a Bible," Kate says. "This does not point to Daniel any more than it points to Megan Walsh."

"I am not saying that it points to Daniel," I reply, patience wearing thin. "But you are going to have to accept that it is very likely that someone you know is threatening you, whether you like it or not. I saw a rifle in the church, at the vigil," I go on. "Who owns that one?"

Kate looks at me. Her eyes are guarded. "It's Daniel's."

For a moment, all I can do is gape at her. "Father Daniel owns a weapon?"

"You think only men like Sean own guns?" Kate asks, almost scoffing at me. She is right to scoff. I should know better than that. Still, Daniel would not have struck me as the kind of man to be into shooting. "Plenty of people own rifles around here," Kate goes on. "Sean, William O'Rawe, the Adamses. Maybe even Megan and Patrick, yes. I don't know."

There were plenty of rifles leaning against the wall of the Walsh's house. William O'Rawe was there, too. We still don't know how his wife Florence knew about Kate's injury. I didn't say anything, Kate didn't say anything.

That only leaves Daniel.

To hell with it. "I'm going to see Father Daniel right now."

"I'm coming with you," Kate says.

"No, you aren't," I say sharply. She got to object with her little visit to the graveyard, now it's my turn. "You will lock the door behind me and not go out on your own, do you understand?"

Kate's expression twists into something awful.

"Last night, there was a man outside your house with a rifle," I say, clenching my teeth so that I will not shout.

"He did not do anything. If he wanted to do something, why did he just stand there?"

"You cannot seriously tell me that you are not at least a little bit frightened!"

"Don't you fucking shout at me," she answers.

"I am sorry," I say, trying with all my might not to shake

her. "I didn't want to shout at you. Listen, please stay here. I want you to be safe."

"By hiding in my house?" she hisses.

"You were attacked!" I take a step towards her. "Kate, someone used violence against you, and they were standing outside your house with a rifle last night."

I can see that she is struggling. She wants to protest, but she knows I'm right.

It seems to be physically painful for her, but she nods.

The church lies empty as I walk in. Grey daylight is filtering in through the windows; the ceiling is so high, so high above me. When I look up, it seems to be spinning away from me for a moment. It doesn't exactly make me feel better when I see the rifle, once again leaning carelessly against a wall at the back of the church.

I make for the side door to the left of the altar, hoping to find Daniel behind it, assuming it leads to the sacristy.

When I am no more than three feet away from it, it is suddenly pushed open from the other side, making me jolt backwards. Barely far enough to avoid the collision, Daniel's chest brushing mine before he even realises I am there. Again he freezes, as if in shock. He is right there, right in my face, him and his tall body and long throat and wide innocent brown eyes.

I am breathing hard all of a sudden.

For a moment, I think that so is he.

Then he takes a decided step back, looking me up and down again, and his expression turns stormy.

"You don't seem glad to see me," I say, bluntly. Perhaps this is his tell, that expression. Perhaps he did let it slip that Kate was attacked, and that is why he is shrinking from me.

"Nothing could be more untrue," he says quietly, evidently battling some complicated emotions that I cannot decipher.

"I am not so very glad to see you seem to make a habit

155

of leaving this lying around." I jerk my head at the rifle. "Any good shooting lately?"

Daniel's brow furrows. "What, you mean that old thing?"

"Correct me if I am wrong, but as far as I can tell, that old thing happens to be a working firearm."

"I will lock it up right away," he says, and I follow him into the sacristy, where he locks the rifle into a cabinet. It is a small but light room, comfortably cluttered, a large desk at the centre and dark shelves with many books along the walls.

"Listen, word about Kate's injury got out," I say. "I didn't tell anyone, and neither did Kate."

"She's already phoned me about this," he replies, furrowing his brow as he puts the key to the cabinet into his pocket. His movements are erratic. "I told her I hadn't said a word."

He looks at me when I say no more. "You don't believe me."

There is something to his voice. A tremor. As if he was nervous.

"Why are you nervous?" I ask.

"I'm not nervous," Father Daniel lies.

"Your hands are shaking," I point out. "Are you lying to me?"

He keeps looking at me, that stormy expression back on his face even as he tries, desperately tries, to keep his voice even: "This may be hard for you to believe, but so are yours."

I glance down.

He is right.

God-fucking-damnit!

"How do I know?" I ask. "How do I know that you are telling the truth? Who blabbed if it wasn't you?"

He shakes his head. He is tall, our priest. "You will have to have faith."

"Do you?"

"What?" He turns away, to his desk, shuffling with the many papers and Post-it notes on top of it.

"Do you still have faith? Considering you are no longer celibate."

His fingers still on the desk. He closes his eyes. "She told you."

"It was difficult to miss," I say. "You're not subtle, Father Daniel."

He flinches. "I'm not?" he asks, trying to smile. Trying to make light of it.

"No," I say, stepping a little closer. I can smell his eau de cologne and his sweat and something which could be incense.

"You'd perhaps be surprised, Jannis," he says, turning back to me.

"Why?" I ask, because I have to know. I cannot just take this on faith. I need to know if he has a reason to want to hurt Kate. If he knew that she wasn't in love with him. "Why are you risking your vocation, your career, your life, for someone who does not even love you back?"

He visibly staggers.

"You goddamn fucking arsehole," he says, but he says it quietly. He closes his eyes. There is anger in his face and beneath it the barely contained sadness of someone who is about to break into tears.

I can feel myself deflate. The guilt hits me with the sudden strength of a bottle to the head, glass shattering against your skull, your body slowly sinking to the floor. I open my mouth. But I do not know what to say.

"Why are you still standing there?" Daniel asks, still speaking quietly. "Is there anything else you would like to add to my humiliation?"

There isn't.

"We have to find out who blabbed," I say.

He laughs, silently. "Get out."

I do.

Kate's car isn't there.

I panic before I have even parked the rental. Jumping out, I run for the door. She left. She left on her own. She might be lying somewhere, head split open, bleeding out while I was arguing with Daniel.

Once inside the house, I call her name, giving in to the irrational hope that she will answer. Needless to say, there is no reply. I check all the rooms. It takes me two sweeps through the kitchen until I notice the bright yellow Post-it note on the counter.

You goddamn fucking arsehole

K

Daniel must have called while I was driving back. He must have confronted her.

Cursing in German, because it is so much more satisfying, I reach for my phone and dial her mobile. It rings. And rings. I pace. And pace. "Come on." It rings. Keeps ringing. I keep pacing. Front of the kitchen. Back of the kitchen. "Come on!"

Click. Her voicemail.

I curse, louder this time, and try again. This time, it goes straight to voicemail. Staring at the note, I run my hand through my grey locks, my movements erratic, scratching across my beard, fuck, fuck. Where could she have gone?

Daniel. Maybe she went to the church, to talk things through with him.

I am ready to grasp at straws. Even though he is the last person that I want to face right then, I reach for my phone.

Do I even have his number?

No, I fucking don't.

Back out. Back into the car. I need to find her.

Back to him.

"She isn't here, Jannis."

"Where could she have gone?" I ask, back in the sacristy.

"I don't know. She didn't say anything to me."

I want to grab him by the shoulders and shake him. Kate out there on her own with someone out to get her. "There was someone at the house last night," I say, hands clenched to fists. "Someone came to her house with a rifle."

Daniel goes pale. He glances at the cabinet that contains his rifle.

Then he takes out the key. "Okay," he says. "Let's go."

"Where?" I ask, matching the brisk pace he sets.

"I don't know. But we're going to find her."

We check the graveyard first, but there is nothing but glistening snow and tall headstones and the sound of the branches of the ancient yew tree, cracking under the white weight.

I look out over the white graveyard and the white mountains beyond, the church and the ancient stone walls no more than pale ghosts. The sky is as white as the snow and the clouds seem to be closing in on us, fog wafting up the hill, turning wood and stone and flesh into grey shadows. It draws out my fears, closing in on me like the fog and the clouds until I am blinded by it.

"Where could she be?" Daniel asks next to me. "She could have gone to her practice?"

"What for?"

"To get that scalpel on her desk to cut your throat?" he suggests.

It reveals a streak of dry humour I had not noticed in him before. "Very funny," I say.

"Well, do you have a better idea?"

I look at the wooden cross at our feet with Alice Walsh's name on it. Her memorial sits right under the yew tree, on top of the hill. There are so many fresh flowers and even more red graveyard candles. Everyone seems to have been allowed to bring something, everyone except Kate. There is even a wreath already, made of white lilies and tall gladioli.

Elizabeth

Tessa
Adams
William
Florence
O'Rawe
Girls and boys come out to play
With heartfelt condolences

"Florence O'Rawe," I say, our breaths turning to white clouds in front of our mouths. "How did she know? How did she know about the injury?"

"I don't know," Daniel replies, fixing his gloves. At least he is wearing gloves, and a sensible coat. His thin face is turning raw in the cold. "I don't know," he repeats, and suddenly, he is taking off. "But we're going to find out."

We go to the practice first to check, but there seems to be nobody there. Then Daniel navigates me to the home of Florence and William O'Rawe. They live in a large house off the side road of a side road in the middle of a forest of tall, dark pine trees. Daniel rings the doorbell, but no one answers. They sky is an oppressive dark grey, as if the sun had no intention of ever rising today.

"That's a bit unusual that no one's in," Daniel says while I try to glance in through one of the front windows. They live in a very nice house, the two of them, three floors and a private driveway and more land at the back than any one person should reasonably have. "Not Florence, she should be at the library, but William…"

I think I may be looking into their sitting room. "Would it be normal for them to be flying the Irish flag in there?" I ask.

Daniel shrugs. "Will took Florence's name at the wedding, and he hasn't exactly been quiet about his loyalties. Pat's his best friend, and he was involved with the IRA in the past. I think the only reason why they are not putting up a flagpole is to spare his mother's feelings. Staunch unionist, Elizabeth is. It's relatively quiet here, usually, especially in the winter, but you should see the Mountains come July. People paint the pavements in the colours of the Irish flag or the Union Jack for the Battle of the Boyne. It gets fairly intense for a while."

"I know," I say. "I remember when I came here for the

first time, Kate picked me up from the airport, and we were stopped by the police because they wanted to make sure we weren't smuggling weapons. Apparently, both unionists and republicans have come to Germany for weapons in the past." I look around the quiet woods, the tall mountains, the many many sheep. "When you look around, you wouldn't believe that people paint their pavements here, would you?"

"There are even two newspapers," Daniel says as he presses the doorbell once more. "To each their own. At least they can both be sold side by side at the Coop."

That is when something catches my eye. On the holly bush by the front door, to our left. It is a bit of fabric, I think, as I step closer, dread settling at the pit of my stomach. It looks suspiciously like a bit of fabric from Kate's new coat.

"This is odd," Daniel repeats, "maybe he's out with Neighbourhood P—"

That is when we hear the shot.

"It came from the back of the house!" I shout, whirling around, and start running.

The garden is white and cold and the ground is slippery and I almost fall, twice, before I finally manage to circle the house.

William O'Rawe is standing in the centre of the clearing, holding the rifle propped up against his shoulder, taking aim.

Aiming at a tin can on a tree stump.

I come to a halt. Daniel follows me. William O'Rawe puts the rifle across his shoulder when he spots us. "Ah, it's you. Come to help me with target practice?" He grins. He is in his late fifties, but still very attractive. And knows it, too?

"Is this yours?" I ask him sharply.

"My mother's," he explains. He is wearing a tartan scarf, Irish silk according to the label. "And what business is it of yours?"

"Had it last night already, did you?" I ask.

"No, it was at my mother's," he replies.

"Why are you shooting at tin cans, William?" Daniel asks.

"Well, we'd better be prepared, hadn't we?" William straightens his shoulders. "We're protecting this neighbourhood now. And we're not going to let them put up another border, either."

"Jesus, William," Daniel admonishes, throwing up both hands.

"What?" he asks. "You're just going to let them walk all over you?"

"On the side of the weak and the needy and those who protest in peace," Daniel replies. "Right now, I am on Kate's side. We are looking for her. What is that bit of fabric doing on your holly bush, William?"

William O'Rawe stares at Daniel. "Sean told me you picked her side at the graveyard. You know that the police have not made any more arrests, don't you? You know that the only reason they let her go was because they didn't have sufficient evidence to charge her. You have to admit, it could have been her. The police don't think so, because she's a woman. They always get away with everything, because it's them who have all the power in the end, isn't it? It's them, they have the wee ones or they don't, they say it's their bodies as if we had no part in it at all, and Kate's always been like that, she's always been like that. When Florence went to see her about having children, Florence came back and said she didn't want to have any anymore, and it was her right, and it was all that bitch telling her..."

"Was Kate here?" Daniel repeats. "That's all I want to know."

William shrugs. "Sure, she came by just now. Her coat caught on the bush. Can't say I'm sorry. She wanted to know where the twins are living. You know, the twins, the cottage where they live is my mother's—"

"Thank you," Daniel says. He takes me by the wrist. "We'll go then."

William O'Rawe is still holding the rifle. "You do that," he says. "And you tell her to watch her back. Wouldn't want anything to happen to her now, would we?"

The air in the car is warm and dry. Daniel's long fingers lie pale and firm on the steering wheel. "You see," he says. "She's fine."

I nod. "It's so like her. Going off on her own like that. Drives me mad."

"Well, yes, she'll do that to you."

His phone is on shuffle. A song comes on. It is a number from a musical, an off-off-Broadway one, none of the big productions.

I glance down at the screen. "I saw that," I say. "At the Fringe."

"Secret thespian?" he asks.

"I go every year."

"I lock up the church every August and spend the summer at the Fringe myself. Where do you stay, though? Hotels are insane in the summer."

"I am loaded," I say, dead serious.

He glances at me.

"Bed and breakfast thirty minutes from the Royal Mile," I concede. "Why, where do you stay?"

"With my parents," he says matter-of-factly.

"Explains the accent," I comment.

"I have been told it makes me sound very sexy," he says.

I say nothing.

He glances at me.

Then he looks back at the road.

The cottage sits by the ocean road. This is exactly where the Mourne Mountains look like the perfect mixture of Norwegian fjords and the coast of southern France. It is a truly beautiful stretch of coast, right by the Rostrevor Forest with its walks and climbs and trees. There is no snow on the ground here, not so close to the water. The sun sits bright and white behind the thick clouds that stretch out over the sea.

It is built of grey stone like most of the houses, and has those vertical white blinds I have never seen anywhere else but around the Mountains of Mourne, where they seem to be mandatory. It looks cosy enough from the outside.

The door is opened by the young man I saw crying in the church. It feels like such a long time ago. He was the one who said he was sorry, to his sister, just before they left the church.

He is not crying right now, but he looks like he might have done quite a bit of it over the past few days. He is wearing tight black trousers, leggings really, a black shirt and large red Angry Birds slippers. His eyes are wide and dark, like a doe's, and his hair is standing up in all imaginable directions. He looks like the opposite of an angry bird.

"Hi, Enda," Father Daniel says, smiling politely. "We were told Kate was with you?"

The young man nods mutely, then motions for us to come inside. The cottage looks as if it was outfitted by an elderly lady in the 1950s, and then no one made any changes to it ever again: floral beige wallpaper, beige carpets, antique closets, decorative porcelain plates on every available surface and rose patterns wherever you look.

Enda returns to the sitting room, where he kicks off his slippers before he sits down on a chintz sofa next to his sister. This must be Betha. The sofa barely registers his weight. There isn't much to register. Betha is wearing black tights, skirt and a blouse, including a lot of neon-coloured bands holding her hair up in a bun. She is wearing rainbow and pro-choice badges. Her arms are crossed in front of her chest as she watches us come in. "We're busy here."

She tilts her head at the coffee table, which seems to be an old seafarer's chest. And there sits Kate. On the chest in front of the twins. She turns around. Her eyes widen as she sees us. "You two mates all of a sudden?" she asks through clenched teeth.

"No," Daniel and I answer almost simultaneously. The young man and woman, Enda and Betha, stare at us. The tension does not escape them. How could it? All three of us staring at each other, everyone evidently wanting to say or do something but none having the balls to go through with it.

Kate turns back to the teenagers on the couch, shifting uncomfortably, Betha with her back as ramrod straight as if she was in an interrogation room, and Enda with his legs tucked in under him. I believe that he does not realise that he is fiddling with a hole in his very colourful sock, making it larger by the moment. Maybe that is his nervous tic.

"Should they be listening to this?" Betha asks. Her voice

is firm and dark. She seems suspicious of all three of us. Her most impressive scowl is reserved for Daniel, however.

Kate presses her lips into a thin line. Then she straightens: "They are all right. We just have things to talk about. Daniel, maybe we could go back to yours after this."

The twins exchange glances. They look a right pair, the two of them, fresh-faced young people wearing rainbow flags and Remain and Border Poll buttons in this old cottage where every table is covered in doilies and every cushion is mustard yellow with a pattern of red roses, kept in suspiciously good shape.

Kate turns back to the twins. "As I was telling you, I have been receiving threatening messages. A few nights ago, there was a knock on the door, but when I opened it, no one was there. And last night, someone came to the house with a rifle."

Betha's eyes narrow.

"So, you see," Kate goes on, "I have reason to be concerned. And I believe that it may have something to do with Alice Walsh. Which is why I am here. She was your friend, wasn't she?"

Betha snorts. "We were the only ones not making her life a living hell, that's for sure."

Kate leans in. "What do you mean?"

Betha glances at her brother. He seems to be silently pleading with her. She shakes her head. He nods. She shakes her head again. He nods more fiercely. She crosses her arms, shakes her head once more and turns back to us. "If she didn't tell you, it's not for us to say."

Enda bites his lip. I glance at him. The hole in his sock has grown very, very big.

"Are you sure you cannot tell us?" Kate asks softly.

Betha shakes her head again.

But then Enda speaks up, and for a moment, I am surprised to find that he can talk. "Maybe we should, though," he says. "For her." And he looks horribly forlorn.

"Fuck," Betha says, scrubbing a hand across her face, her mouth. She gets up and walks to the kitchen sink. While she splashes water onto her face, Kate turns to Enda. "Do you think it would help with the murder investigation? Have you talked to the police about it?"

"Not about this," Enda replies, looking increasingly nervous. He keeps glancing at the door. I wonder why.

"You can tell me," Kate says gently. "I'm a doctor. I'm very good at keeping secrets."

It is Betha who answers, from the kitchen sink. "I mean, maybe we can tell her." She turns around to face us. She is staring straight at Kate. "Because it was you who helped her, right? With the abortion?"

A shadow passes over Kate's face even as I stand up straighter. They know. "How do you know that?" Kate asks.

Betha shrugs. "She told us."

"We had to pry it out of her," Enda corrects gently.

"Alice Walsh told you that she was pregnant?" Kate asks. "She told you about the abortion?"

"She did not seem to have anyone else to talk to," Enda says, still sounding miserable. "She seemed so ashamed."

"Is that why you're receiving death threats?" Betha asks, voice sharp. "Because you helped her?"

"Death threats?" Enda looks at Kate, shocked.

But Kate merely nods. "I believe so, yes."

Betha scoffs. "That's not right. That's just not right."

"If we tell them, we should tell them now, Betha," Enda says.

She throws up her hands. "Fine. Fine, her schoolmates were picking on Liz, on Alice, because she was queer and they didn't like it."

Kate and I exchange astonished glances.

"She was... queer?" Kate asks. "As in, she loved women?"

"Well, she didn't say it in so many words," Betha says, and those words seem to hurt. They seem to hurt her very deeply. "But I think I could tell. And so could her classmates."

"But the pregnancy..." I begin, unsure of how to continue.

"Maybe it was a praying-the-gay-away thing," Enda says, staring into the distance.

"Women do that a lot when they first suspect they fancy other girls," Betha explains. "Sleeping with a man. As if they just haven't tried hard enough yet, being heterosexual. As if they need a penis inside of them, to know for sure."

"You know this for certain?" I ask. "That Alice Walsh identified as queer?"

This time, it is for Betha to bite her lip. She looks just like her brother when she does that. "No," she admits. Again, it seems to be painful just to speak the words: "I wanted to ask her. We were supposed to have dinner, her and me, the day she was murdered." She swallows. "Goes without saying we never did."

We are quiet for a moment. Then she continues, trying so hard to make her voice sound anything but raw: "So no, we don't know anything for sure. But I am pretty sure. She as good as admitted it. When she told us about the priest."

She jerks her head at Daniel.

I feel Kate stiffen. "What?"

Enda looks at his feet. Betha raises both eyebrows. Some part of her is enjoying this, some righteous teenage part that would also rather be angry than hurt. "Do you mean you don't know? You didn't suspect?"

"Suspect what?" I ask. "Out with it."

She rolls her eyes. "Your priest. He's gay. And Liz knew."

No one speaks. No one makes a sound. No one even moves a muscle.

Then Daniel starts. "I have to go," he says and walks out, without looking at anyone.

The door closes behind him. It rings loud in the silence.

"She went to confession a lot when she started having… doubts," Enda says. "He helped her. Shared his own doubts. He encouraged her to do what she felt was right, with regards to the baby, too." He glances at Betha. As if there is more to say.

I look at Kate. She has not stirred.

Am I wrong, or does she even seem… a little relieved? Underneath the hurt? "There was something else," Enda says. He takes one last look at Betha, then he turns to Kate: "We might know something. About the father."

"Her father?"

"No, the father of the baby."

Kate leans in. "Enda, this is so very important, so please think carefully. Did she tell you who it was?"

And he shakes his head. "She only said it was a friend of her father's. She said it was horribly inappropriate, but she was so desperate, so full of doubts, and he offered, and was so kind and understanding about it, and then she took him up on it. She thought it would be easier with an experienced man. And it couldn't be someone from school. They hated her in school."

A friend of her father's. If there was any relief in Kate's face, it is now gone.

"Did the father know?" she asks.

Betha breathes in. Then out. "She hadn't told anyone yet, not when we last spoke. But she wanted to."

Kate nods. Then she rises. "Thanks so much, you two," she says. "Have you told the police?"

They nod.

We make our goodbyes, then we leave.

Daniel is standing outside. He is leaning against his car. He looks very pale.

We are having very strong drinks at Kate's house. We are all sitting in Kate's sitting room, Kate on the floor with her back against the coffee table, facing the back door, Daniel and I on the sofa. I am awkwardly holding my gin and tonic. Daniel is clutching his glass hard, as if he might want to crush it. Kate has already downed hers.

The conversation so far has been stilted. Perhaps dominated by silence would be a more apt description.

"Did you know that Alice Walsh had been sleeping with a friend of her father's?" Kate asks him.

"No, I didn't know," he says. "Kate, listen, I am sorry."

She shakes her head. I believe I was right when I thought that she looked relieved, underneath the hurt, when she first heard he was gay. I think I know why, because I have known her for twenty years. If she had been Daniel's one and only, her responsibility to him would have felt larger, her guilt at not loving him back the same way he did heavier.

This way, she does not need to feel guilty for not loving him. She can stop asking it of herself.

"I assume you wanted to try it," she says. "You wanted to be sure."

Daniel puts down his glass and buries his face in his hands.

In light of his distress, we have silently agreed to make up and rally for now.

"How about," I suggest, "we focus on what we know

about the case: Alice Walsh told Enda and Betha that a friend of Patrick's was the father of the child she aborted. She had not told him yet, but she had perhaps meant to."

"Do you think she may have gotten around to it? And that was why she was killed?" Kate asks.

"Who would do such a thing?" Daniel says, lowering his hands from his face. He seems to be pulling himself back from a place very far away when his eyes focus on Kate. "Who could it be?"

Kate puts her hands to her lips. "William and Pat are close, of course. Sean could be considered their friend, and he is much closer in age to Alice Walsh than William."

"There were so many men standing outside their house with the neighbourhood protection," I say. "There may be many friends we are not aware of."

"And do we truly think she admitted it to the father of the child?" Father Daniel asks. "She was so ashamed, too ashamed almost to talk to me about it, and I knew that she had been pregnant. She came to speak to me about the abortion. She pretended it was in general terms. She also talked about loving women in general terms, at least to me. Would she tell the friend of her father's?"

"Do either of you know anything about Alice Walsh's taste in men? Did she have any sort of special connection with either Sean O'Doherty or William O'Rawe? Or another friend of her father's?" I ask.

Kate shakes her head. "Not that I'd know, but then again, I wouldn't. I can much more easily imagine it to have been Sean, though. I cannot imagine Alice Walsh having sex with William O'Rawe. He is so much older than her."

"He is attractive in a way," I say "And he had a rifle."

"Do you really think that William O'Rawe, fifty-nine, came down here last night and held a vigil with his mum's rifle?" she scoffs.

"Someone was here. Kate, you are still pretending that there is no real danger. You're still pretending that there is no one out there out to get you, and I don't understand why. Aren't you scared?"

"Are you kidding me?" Kate stares at me. "I am scared shitless."

"Then why…"

"Because women have been scared shitless for far too long! Because being scared won't help!" She is out of breath, looking at us intensely, as if she was willing us to understand just by sheer force of will. "What has it accomplished for you, being worried about me?"

"If I had come with you to the graveyard, you would not have been attacked."

"You cannot protect me," Kate answers.

"I think I can," I insist. "I am stronger, I am—"

"You cannot protect me, because I do not want you to."

"Then why call me?" I ask. "Why call me? What do you want from me?"

"Support," she says, as if it was the easiest answer in the world.

And perhaps it is.

"I do not want you to protect me," Kate says, standing right in front of me. "I want you to support me."

I wish there was anything I could say except what a shit friend I have been. I reach for her. Carefully. As carefully,

Kate leans in. Rests her forehead against my chest. Slowly, I wrap my arms around her shoulders. Scratch her scalp.

"Like that?" I ask quietly.

"Hmhm." She makes a contended noise. "Good start, that."

I rest my head against the top of hers, lowering my hands to rub her shoulders through the fine layer of chequered wool. All the lies, the unspoken and the half-spoken and never-spoken, they fall off of me. It is such a relief to hold her.

"How about that, also helpful?"

"Very."

And she laughs then, quietly. It is the most intimate moment I have had in years. It is so intimate, her hair in my nose, the scent of her shampoo, her compact lithe elegant body breathing, just breathing against mine, that for the briefest moments, I manage to forget that we are not alone.

Until Daniel clears his throat in an intensely awkward way. "I'd better be going," he says, rising to his feet. But instead of leaving, he turns to Kate. "I am very, very sorry, Kate. I should never have… I should have been open from the start. I hope you can find it in yourself to forgive me."

I can feel how deep the breath is that Kate takes before she turns to face him. "Dan," she says, "I wish I could have loved you. Even though I was not what you were looking for. Not really."

Daniel swallows. His expression is as raw now as it was earlier, standing in the freezing cold in the graveyard. "I wish I could have loved you, too," he says before he makes to leave.

I rise to my own feet. "Are you sure you should be driving?"

His voice is very, very dry: "I'm fine." He lifts his glass, to show he has only had two sips.

Kate looks miserable. And so does Daniel. Especially as he takes one last look at me before he goes.

"I think one of us should go after him," Kate says quietly, "and I think it shouldn't be me."

"My thoughts exactly," I say as I separate and follow Daniel out into the hall.

He is just about to put on his sensible coat. His sensible coat, sensible hat, sensible gloves. And yet nothing about this man seems sensible to me. Not the car he drives, not the way he speeds, not the women he chose to sleep with. Not the way his expression is twisted and his voice is raw and his eyes cannot meet mine.

I bury my hands in the pockets of my cardigan. It is soft and warm against my skin. It matches how calm I am feeling. How soft and warm.

"You don't have to go."

"No, trust me, I do," he mumbles, putting on his hat.

I take a hesitant step towards him while he fumbles with his gloves.

"There is nothing," and I make sure to stress the word, "nothing wrong with needing time to figure things out."

"I know," Daniel says, still trying to struggle into his gloves.

"So why don't you stay," I suggest again, taking another step towards him, less tentative this time. It seems ludicrous now, having suspected him. "We could have another drink, take your mind off things. There is a comfy sofa, too. You probably don't want to drink and drive."

He opens his eyes. He looks straight at me. His brown eyes and his stormy expression. His long throat and tall silhouette and the way he swallows. Like he is swallowing down words desperately clawing their way up his throat.

"No," Father Daniel says softly. "No, believe me, I'd rather not stay. It would not be wise. It would only make me realise, ever more clearly, how I have been trying not to commit one sin by trying my hands at a lesser one."

That is when I realise.

What a fucking idiot I have been.

He has been looking at me like that all this time. At me.

And his stormy expression might not be one of hostility.

He is still looking at me.

There is a knock on the door.

Daniel turns around quick as lightning, almost tearing the door open before I can even do so much as move a muscle. "No, Daniel, wa—"

It is a man with a rifle.

It is Sean O'Doherty.

"So I spoke with O'Rawe, and he told me you'd paid him a visit."

Father Daniel has left. Now it is Sean O'Doherty standing in the living room. He is dressed in what to me seems to be an H&M version of combat gear, gratuitous camouflage pattern in all shades of grey, and carrying what appears to be a fairly empty duffle bag. Looking at the two of them, Kate with her suit and the innate elegance of a professional dancer, and Sean in his fake combat suit and inflated arms, I cannot help but wonder once again how the two of them ever ended up in a relationship.

"He said you're sniffing around now. Interfering with the case," Sean continues. "This is exactly the kind of anti-social behaviour Neighbourhood Protection is here to prevent." He crosses his arms in front of his chest. "Listen, I'm sorry to say this, but the community would like both of you to leave."

Kate makes an impatient sound: "Get out, Sean."

"No, I'm serious, Kate. You got to go."

Kate says nothing. She merely raises her eyebrows.

Sean throws up his hands. "See," he says, "I knew you'd be like that." He pulls the duffle bag off his shoulders and throws it onto the coffee table, scattering the letters, our lists. "Pack your things, Kitty. You're leaving."

"The hell I am." I wish that she would sound outraged at least. But instead, Kate's voice is tired. She looks so tired of fighting.

"Listen, you can come sleep at my place for the night, and then I'll drive you up to Newry, and we'll find you a hotel," Sean insists.

"You were significantly less kind at the graveyard," Kate replies.

He narrows his eyes. "Stop being so selfish!"

"Stop saying I'm selfish!"

"No, seriously," he goes on, jabbing his finger at her. "You were selfish when we were together, you were selfish at the graveyard, and you're being selfish now! Just accept some goddamn fucking help when it's offered."

Kate is going increasingly pale. I see how it takes effort for her to draw herself up, to turn her expression into one of stone, not allowing for any of her doubts to show. "It's very nice of you to offer, Sean, but I don't need your help. I'm fine where I am."

Sean tilts his head at me. "You think he will protect you?" He even laughs a little as he says it.

Why, thank you, Sean.

"Shut up, Sean," Kate repeats.

He turns to me, ignoring her entirely. "You think you can? Mate, you're wrong."

"Leave him alone," Kate insists, taking an aggressive step towards Sean. He goes on ignoring her, looking at me.

"Listen, I need to know that she's safe, because I care about her. So you tell me she'll be safe for tonight, and that you'll both be out of here tomorrow, and I'll be out of here. Not trying to stake any claims where the land's already been ploughed."

"Will you listen to me?" Kate asks, desperation tinging her voice now. "Sean, listen to me."

He does not budge, still looking at me. "You will leave in the morning, won't you? Go to Newry?"

She stares at him, her arms shaking, her mouth hanging open. Her hands are clenched into fists.

And it is terrible. It is so terrible watching her trying to speak to him, looking at him, and all he does is keep looking at me. I search and hold Sean's gaze, then I say: "Kate is right there, Sean."

"I'm not talking to her," Sean says.

That is when Kate loses it. She takes the two remaining steps, grabs Sean's chin and forcefully turns it towards her. "I am serious," she hisses. "You get out. You get out now!"

And there is something. It might be the tremor in her voice, the tears glistening in her eyes, or the red patches of anger on her skin.

Whatever it is, it makes him look at her.

"Come on, Kitty," he says, suddenly quiet. "Come on, you got to go. I'm serious."

She shakes her head. She lets him go. Pushes him away. "Get out!"

Sean takes up his duffle bag, his rifle, glances at me one last time, nods, and then he is gone.

The moment she has heard the front door fall shut, Kate sinks down onto the sofa. She buries her face in her hands. Her shoulders start shaking.

I sit down next to her. Wrap an arm around her.

"That fucking arsehole," she hiccups, between her tears, between trying to wipe them off more quickly than they come. "That fucking arsehole made me cry. I couldn't hold them back, and he only left because he can't fucking handle it when someone cries…"

I pull her closer. Put my lips against her temple. "It's all right. He's gone now."

"Maybe we should go," she says. She's hiccupping. "Hotel. Newry. Maybe he's right. Maybe we should get out of here."

I pull her towards me. She puts her head on my shoulder.

"You can lean on me, too, you know," she says.

I nod. Slowly, I lower my head. I put it on top of hers.

We sit like this for a while. Until she is no longer shaking in my arms. Until she reaches out to wipe her face. There is no music on in the background, there are only the inky sounds of the encroaching night.

"Why do you think he came?" I ask.

"Because he's an arsehole," she replies. "Thinks he's all important with that Neighbourhood Watch crap."

"No, I mean…" I hesitate.

Kate looks at me. "What?"

"Maybe he knows more than we do."

"Like what?"

"Maybe he knows who has been threatening you. Maybe he thinks that something's going to happen."

"Or maybe it was him all along," she says. "Maybe this is his way of revenge."

No music.

Only the inky sounds of the encroaching night.

Only our breaths in the darkness.

"Are you upset about Daniel?" I ask her. We are still in the sitting room. Neither of us has bothered to turn on the lights.

She shakes her head. "No," she replies. "I suspected. Besides, it's time I stopped dating men who aren't good for me." She is holding onto the soles of her feet, knees drawn into her chest. "Makes you think, doesn't it." She stares at the lists and letters on the table. "Time's precious."

"You can still be upset," I tell her. "Even if it's all right."

She shrugs. "What good would that do?"

Then she looks at me. "I'm not upset about the way you look at him."

I stop. I start. "What?"

She smiles, even though it looks a little watery. "Well, am I wrong?"

"How did you know? How do you even know that I fancy... well..."

"Men?"

"Both!"

"I've had my suspicions."

"When?" I sit up. "How?"

She laughs. "Oh, just since we first met."

I stare at her, wide-eyed. "I was hitting on you when we first met!"

She grins. "Well, I figured you went for both. You were also making eyes at the waiter, don't you remember? He was very fit. Much fitter than you, really. It was a bit embarrassing, let me tell you."

And then we are both laughing all of a sudden. It is the only thing to do in the silence and the darkness of the night that is coming.

We make a quick dinner, then we do the washing up. I ask Kate whether she wants to stay at a hotel tonight.

She shakes her head.

"Let's decide tomorrow. I'm knackered."

I nod. Then I glance out of the kitchen window.

It is late. It is dark.

They might be back.

Kate follows my gaze. Quickly, I look back at the washing up, but it is too late. She has already risen to her feet. Already turned off the light and stepped up to the kitchen window.

"Can you see anything?" I ask quietly, still tasting the sweet soft icing of the carrot cake on my tongue.

She stares.

And stares.

And stares.

"Kate?" I ask.

Finally, she shakes her head. "No, there is nothing."

I join her by the window. I can see nothing but the mountains and the moor and the trees. There is no movement. No rifle. No silhouette.

"Maybe they're not coming tonight," Kate whispers.

I am about to nod when we hear the crashing sound.

It is coming from the bedroom.

23:29

The brick has shattered the window. The glass is spread out all over the floor, the bed, the blanket and pillows.

Kate's and my fingers intertwine as she reaches for the piece of paper that has been fastened to it.

There shall be one law for the native and for the stranger who sojourns among you.

The words blur in front of my eyes. Kate calls me by my name.

"What does this mean?" I ask.

"It means," she says, sounding angry and worried and afraid, "that now they're after you, too."

Are you here about Alice Walsh?

Oh. Oh. You're not? What is it about, then?

I think I should be getting Will.

No? All right. Of course.

No, I'm a little... Things like that don't happen here. They just don't happen here.

You're saying Kate is being threatened? I didn't realise. No, I didn't. That is terrible. Truly terrible.

She was attacked? Goodness me. Goodness.

What do you mean, how did I know about the attack? I didn't know until you just told me.

Oh.

Oh.

Well.

I...

She told you I had come by with the casserole, then. Well, I didn't know what else to do for her, I figured she'd...

She doesn't eat lamb? She's a vegetarian now? Oh, that's good to know. Good to know.

Maybe I should get William after all.

All right, no, no, it's all right. I wouldn't know where he is, anyway. Always in and out, that one. Even before Neighbourhood Protection.

I can tell you how I know of the attack. Of course I can. William told me.

How did he know? Oh, well, wait, let me think...

Goodness me, I don't know. What did he say?

I truly cannot remember, Detective. I'm so sorry. I just don't...

I should take my time, you say? Of course. Of course. I'll take my time... give it a proper think. Yes, a proper think.

Let's see. It was yesterday. I came home from my lunch break. To have lunch. Obviously. I came home, and William was there, and he looked shaken, and he told me his mother had been over. That's odd. It's more than odd, actually. I thought he was pulling my leg. His mother never comes over. But he claimed she'd told him about Kate's injury.

Did I believe him?

Why wouldn't I believe my husband?

That's not what you asked, I know.

I didn't...

I didn't know whether to believe him or not. He's been so... Well. He's been...

Well. I don't know. Maybe he's always been like that.

I didn't know. I just knew that Kate wasn't well, and that

everyone is saying she murdered Alice Walsh, and I realised then that I found the idea absolutely ludicrous. That's when I realised. Everyone is saying it, that it was her, and that they have to do something about it if the police won't.

Who's everyone?

Oh. Oh, you know.

Just.

Everyone.

Day 5

SUNDAY 6TH JANUARY 2019

STATEMENT
DETECTIVE CONSTABLE NORAH BAILEY INTERVIEWING (DOOR-
TO-DOOR)
BETHA O'REILLY
2 COLLEGE RD
GLASHEEN
CORK
T12 ACP5

We came up to visit Alice. As in, Enda and me. He is my twin brother. Yep, twins. Very special and all that.

No, it is. It is special. But that isn't what we are here to talk about, are we? We are here to talk about Liz.

You know what is funny? What is so very funny? Is that we haven't known each other long. Liz and I. Liz and Enda and I. We only met in the summer. She was in Cork for it, I don't even know why, really. She wanted a break from her parents, I think, and they wouldn't let her travel any further on her own? I don't even know.

Yes, that is where we met. On the beach.

How?

Coincidence. Don't talk to me about fate. So silly. We got lucky, that's all.

How lucky we got.

Is it better, do you think? Is it better to have known someone for a little while than not to have known them at all?

I wouldn't. Change anything. I wanted to know her. She wanted to know me.

We wanted everything.

She wasn't happy at home. No, she really wasn't. That was obvious from the start. She hated her mum. And her dad, he was completely mad.

What do I mean by that?

If he was ever violent towards her? No, God no. She said she was a daddy's girl. Yeah, she really did say that. He was super protective of her.

But he was also… I don't know. He didn't seem right to me. There was something there in his past, I think. The Troubles. I don't know what exactly, Liz never said. So he was very protective of her. He would have killed someone if they did anything to her, I'm pretty sure. And he was so easily disappointed. Liz said he hated her mum, because she'd tried to abort her. Plain hated her. She said that's what turned her mum into such a bitch.

Sorry.

I'm sorry.

Liz could do no wrong in his eyes, of course. She always got away with everything. And he took her with him on hunting trips and stuff, with his friends.

That's how she met the father of the baby.

Did her father know?

I don't know. I don't think so.

Dutifully, we report the new letter to the police, as well as the brick. Detective Sergeant Cahill comes down to the house before dawn. She looks very worried and intensely tired and a little suspicious. She glances at the letter. Then she takes out her notebook, as if trying to verify something.

I wonder what that could be, but the Detective Sergeant does not seem to find what she is looking for, closing her notebook once more while muttering under her breath before she tells us that it might be wise to leave the village. Check into a hotel for a couple of nights.

Once she has left, we sit at the small kitchen table, watching the sun rise above the mountains outside the window. Kate is wearing a dressing-gown, I am still in yesterday's sweater. Neither of us has slept much. We are both cradling a mug of tea, hoping the caffeine will revive us a little.

"How long have you known?" she asks suddenly, seamlessly continuing a conversation cut short by the arrival of the police. "About you... fancying both."

I shrug. "You just know, don't you? You look at someone and you know that you want them."

I am pretending that my heart isn't aching while I say this.

Kate leans back in her chair. "Look at us," she says. "Hell, look at Daniel. Struggling with all this. Young people are much more relaxed about all this, aren't they? They have grown up in this world of peace and relative wealth and with all the rights in the world. Abortion, being gay…"

"Bisexual," I correct her.

She runs her fingers along the rim of her mug. The bags sit heavily under her eyes. "Well, either way, they wouldn't date dickheads like Sean. Or priests."

"Alice slept with a friend of her father's." I think of the man with the rifle. I think of the letters. "We shouldn't stay here. There must be somewhere affordable to stay in Newry. Just for a few days. Give the police a chance to arrest a suspect."

"Yes," Kate says. "We'll pack our bags and spent the night in Newry," Kate says. Then she looks at me. "But first, we have to do one more thing."

"Like what?"

"Go to mass."

"To mass?"

"Well, we can't just go now, when we're so close to finding out who's behind this."

I am staring at her as if she has gone mad. "What?"

"We need to go to mass," she says. "Everyone will be there, won't they?" she says. She seems excited as she makes for the sitting room.

"Yes, I guess," I say, getting up to follow her. "Everyone who's a Catholic, anyway."

"Then we will find the person who threw that brick."

"How?" I ask. "Kate, what's going on?"

She picks up the latest letter. "They rather showed their hand with this one, wouldn't you say?"

It takes me a moment to realise what she is saying. "It's handwritten."

She nods triumphantly. "They must have been in a hurry."

Kate is properly grinning now. "What do you think, the red suit? Before I have to get back into the lab coat tomorrow?"

"Perfect," I reply. "And then to Newry."

She nods. "I'll go get dressed."

"Better find something smarter to wear, too," she says as she leaves the kitchen. "Wouldn't want me to outshine you when we are going to see Father Daniel."

Very wisely, I do not say anything.

All I do is flip her the finger.

Our plan is simple: before mass, we will convince Daniel to include a little interactivity in today's service. He will have to ask everyone to write down a few words, say he will use the notes in the memorial service he is surely planning; he has to ask everyone to write as clearly as possible, preferably in capital letters, for better legibility, of course. This way, we will have a beautiful sample against which to compare the most recent missive.

And perhaps we might even be given a hint about the identity of the man Alice Walsh slept with. He may be there. He may write something down that gives him away, even if he doesn't realise it.

Daniel, however, seems not very well pleased with our idea. "That's deceit," he says as all three of us stand in the sacristy, Daniel, with arms crossed and incapable of looking either of us in the eye. Instead he frowns at the dust collecting on top of the shelves in the rectory. He mumbles something about Tessa not doing her job properly these past few weeks.

"Right," Kate says. "And we all know that's just not your thing."

"It's actually not, you know," he protests. "I was terrible at pretending not to be sleeping with you."

"That is true," I confirm.

He glares at me. Actually glares. I didn't think he was capable.

"Look, it's not technically a lie," Kate tries. "You will actually use them in a memorial service. It's just that they'll be taking a bit of a detour first."

"We need them for a couple of hours, maybe three," I add.

Daniel shakes his head. He looks a little too defeated for my taste. "I thought I was through with lying."

"What's one more time for a worthy cause?" I ask cheerfully.

His expression does not match my cheer. "There is something about you, Jannis, and I am not sure if it does not rub me the wrong way."

"Shame," Kate says innocently. "He speaks so highly of you."

"Fuck off," Daniel and I say at just about the same time. She suppresses a pointed grin, then turns to Daniel. "You owe me. For telling me you loved no one but me, no one, no one, no one."

He gives a painful smile. It makes me ache. "Repaying a lie with another lie?"

"Very Old Testament of me, right?" Kate asks happily. "Eye for an eye."

"When will it end?" Daniel mumbles, looking at the floor.

My heart goes out to him. I want to tell him that one can tell the truth and come out of it alive. More alive, even.

"The truth can be said," I tell Daniel. "You can say it."

He is still staring at the floor. "Then everything will change," he says.

"Yes," I say simply.

He closes his eyes. "Don't worry, I'll do you your little favour. Now let me get ready in peace. And find some pens and paper, which I assume you didn't think to bring."

In fact, we did not.

When the service begins, everyone is here.

The church feels different during the day, and when it is filled with worshippers in their Sunday dress. The stained-glass windows are lit with the pale light of a cold winter morning. Everyone looks sharp, as if thrown into focus. Wrinkles are deeper, exhaustion starker, lips paler, white shirts glaringly bright.

Megan and Patrick Walsh sit in the front row. Megan did not take a single look at us, but she did not ask for us to be removed, either. Patrick Walsh glanced our way. His gait is unstable. They are both in their best Sunday dress.

In the pew behind them sit William and Florence O'Rawe.

Tessa Adams is also there, but she keeps to the back. Maybe she is worried about being spotted by Father Daniel, who might have words with her about the dust on the shelves in the rectory. Her mother is not here. She would be a Protestant, of course. Then again, Tessa might be, too? Sean O'Doherty isn't here, either, I realise, and curse silently.

There is also a large group of strangers assembled in the church this Sunday. A few of Alice Walsh's classmates are back. They are standing with three adults, who I suppose may be their teachers. Horrendous crimes tend to drive people back to mass. No one is on their phone, which surprises me a little, until I remember that there is no signal at the church. Most of the congregation is doing their very best not to look Kate in the eye. I am afraid her practice may not exactly be overrun with patients tomorrow, either.

I am glad we are leaving tonight.

Father Daniel looks nervous as he steps in front of his congregation. He keeps glancing at me, as if to make it absolutely obvious to every single person in this church that we have been plotting something. I wish I could be annoyed by this, but now that it no longer involves a secret affair with Kate and thus no longer puts her at risk, I cannot help but find it endearing. He stutters his way through most of the appropriate words as he suggests that everyone take a moment, after partaking in the Holy Communion, to write down a few words for Alice. He even manages to point in the direction of the slips of paper and the pens he has placed at the far end of the first row of pews. He also strongly implies the slips of papers will be used at a memorial service, and that everyone should make sure to put down their names on the paper, so that they can be contacted and asked for permission should their words play a part in the final service. It is simultaneously the most awkward and the most charming speech I have witnessed in at least a couple of years. People are already fidgeting. I attempt to establish eye contact with Daniel, lest he forget that we talked about people having to write in capital letters. I even mouth the words to him.

When he sees me do this, I am fairly sure that he very, very nearly rolls his eyes. "And if you could write as clearly as possible, please," he adds. "Capital letters when in doubt. Just to make sure that they are legible. For when they will be read out loud. Might be read out loud. At the memorial service. As I may have already mentioned."

There is some shifting and grumbling among the congregation, but in the end, they all follow their priest's suggestion, especially after Daniel goes first, writing a note before the Holy Communion begins. I watch, making a valiant effort to hide my glee, as the first member of the congregation, William O'Rawe, receives his wafer and then moves on to the slips of paper, reaching for the pen. I watch them, one by one, Florence, Megan, Patrick, face after face, one person after the other, like a line-up of suspects, and it is the same feeling in my gut, the excitement, the nerves, the triumph. This is going to go well. I can just tell.

"You coming?" Kate asks, shaking me from my reverie.

"Coming where?" I ask, confused.

She motions with her head towards the altar. Then she leans in to whisper into my ear, her red suit and black shirt soft against my throat: "Probably not clever to be the only ones seen not to do it."

She is right. That is why I nod. And yet, the terror I feel keeps me rooted to the spot. I have not taken Holy Communion in years. Eight, maybe nine, perhaps even eleven? At a Christmas mass? I cannot remember. All I remember is that I am not allowed to partake in Holy Communion. There are mortal sins I have not confessed. Because by God, I am not only using his name in vain, my mortal sin is standing right there at the altar, offering his congregation their wafers, the holy body of Christ.

I want Daniel. If I cannot say it to his face, I have at least admitted it to myself. It is no longer just a thought, that I may also desire men. It is one specific man. He is standing right there.

What would it be, I wonder as I rise and follow Kate, operating on autopilot. What would it be like to actually do it? Not just to say it? When does something become true? Is it the thought that counts, as the Church would have me believe? Is it the words you say? Or is it not until I have touched another man that it becomes a proper part of my life?

Because I never have. Touched another man. Not like that.

I guess what I am wondering is, as our steps resound on the stone floor of the church aisle, is it too late to turn back?

I shuffle closer to Kate as we advance in the line. Before and behind us, the other churchgoers are keeping their distance.

They are whispering behind our backs.

And then we are already up. Kate goes first. Daniel speaks the blessing. She accepts the wafer and moves on, joining the crowd surrounding the pen and paper.

Daniel looks at me. I look at him.

I desperately want to ask: How do you do it? How do you look at me like that when we are at Kate's house, and now, you are every inch the priest?

But all I do is smile awkwardly. He returns it thinly. "I should not," I cannot help saying, pointing helplessly at the wafer.

"Why not?" Daniel asks.

"Mortal sin," I reply, voice pitched so low that he only he will hear me.

He hesitates. "You know that I cannot give you this now that you have told me."

I almost smile. "A little holier-than-thou after all?"

"No," he says, and it is not until I look closely that I realise his eyes are rimmed red. "Holding onto what is already slipping away from me with all that I have."

I nod, then I turn away. He is right, after all. Suppose somebody overheard us. Suppose somebody told his superiors. That would not go over well, it would end his career.

Daniel takes a deep breath. Then he smiles and turns away from me, to the next member of his congregation. He seems distracted as he hands over the next wafer. He looks back at me, just for a moment.

Slowly, I walk over to the far end of the front pew, where everyone has assembled around the slips of paper, some standing pensively, some scribbling furiously. Kate belongs to the latter group. She looks like she is pouring her heart out to someone who can no longer hear her. My chest aches for her as I reach for a piece of paper and a pen.

Looking at the slip of paper in my hand, it suddenly hits me. Alice Walsh is dead. I did not know her personally, but she was a young woman full of dreams and hopes for the future. Who was still trying to figure out who she was. Who could have been anyone, anything. An architect. A doctor. A lover. A teacher. A mother. She could have lived in a house in the Mourne Mountains, overlooking the sea. She could have moved to Paris and made a life for herself. Or gone on a holiday. Feasting on baguettes and croissants. Italy. Maybe she would have liked Italy. Or Thailand. Or Bali. Australia.

A bar in Seventeen Seventy-Seven, where she could have made a friend for life. Or met a one-night stand. Or just had a good drink and a proper barbecue and a good flirt with the barkeeper.

I am startled out of my thoughts when Father Daniel speaks up again. Quickly, I look up. Kate is taking hold of my arm, steering me back towards our pew. The Holy Communion has been cleared away and everyone has returned to their seats. Daniel is standing in front of us, holding the slips of paper in his hands. He does not seem nervous anymore. In fact, he is smiling.

Maybe this is just wishful thinking, but I believe he may be smiling at me. Either way, I smile back. Life is too short. And he lied for us. He went through with it, even though he did not want to. I appreciate that. Before the day is out, we may know who the culprit is. And we'll be safe in a hotel in Newry. Just now, we may have saved Kate from the worst.

"Thank you, everyone," Daniel says, and it is clear that the official part of mass is over. "I am looking forward to seeing you all again. The next service takes place, as you know, on Wednesday. The church will then also be open for confession."

Shuffling all around. I make to rise, too.

"There is one more thing I should tell you," Daniel goes on.

Everyone settles back down. Daniel glances up at the ceiling. Then he looks at us. He is still smiling. "You will not see me there."

No one is making even the faintest noise. I furrow my brow. He laughs a little. As if he could not believe what he is about to do. What God will watch him do. "I find that I am no longer capable of fulfilling my office." His voice is firm. "God has made me in a way which I only now have realised clearly means that I am not intended to serve Him this way. I realised this because I committed a mortal sin."

I see the car crash coming, but there is nothing I can do but keep my hands on the steering wheel. There are no brakes to hit. All I do is prepare to rise. Because I do not know if Daniel is about to come out to his congregation, and if so, if everyone is going to stay calm and collected or if they are going to attack him where he stands. All I know is that this is his confessional.

And then Daniel says it: "I had an affair. I broke my oath of celibacy."

I rise. I open my mouth, but it is too late. Daniel charges ahead. "I must tell you the truth. This is what I can do for Alice." He looks up at the ceiling. He smiles. "I know you can see me. And I thank you for your trust, Alice, while you were still here with us. For your encouragement. I'd hoped I could encourage you in return."

Then he looks back at us. "For Alice Walsh helped me see something. She helped me see that God makes us all differently."

And then he is looking straight at me. "You must know that I am gay. And that that is how God made me."

"It was you who told me to be honest!"

Daniel is shouting. I am trying to hit the sweet spot between shouting and whispering, and I am failing miserably. "Not like that!" I reply furiously. "Not in front of your entire congregation, including people who walk around with rifles in the night!"

We are back in the rectory, the door slammed shut and locked, the air thick with dust and our voices. I basically used my body as a shield to get Father Daniel away from the congregation and safely into the sacristy. I saw Megan Walsh's face, and Patrick Walsh pale as the wafer, and William O'Rawe with his mouth open and his face turning red, and the only reason why I did not call the police right away was because there was no signal, and because I knew it would take them too long to get here to provide any sort of meaningful protection to the priest. Megan Walsh came very close to assaulting Daniel before we made it into the sacristy. Kate came into the sacristy with us, then used the connecting door to go into the rectory and make sure all doors and windows are locked.

Daniel is struggling out of his *Messgewand*, which I believe is a chasuble in English, followed by his *Stola*, his stole, white and gold. It irks me that I still remember the names for these clothes. I have not been an altar boy in almost thirty years, and yet here they still are, the memories of kneeling and breathing the stale air and the shame, unbearably hot and heavy. Staring up at the high ceilings and feeling like you are nothing, not even worth the dust under your knees.

Daniel tosses his stole onto the chair in front of his impossibly cluttered desk, so many slips of paper, some of them printed, others covered in his handwriting, neat capital letters, Bible quotations, arranged in a sort of mind map. I recognise parts of today's sermons as I reach for him. "What were you thinking?"

"Why do we always end up shouting at each other?" he asks. He has not shaken me off. Not yet.

"Because you keep doing incredibly stupid things!" I have not let him go. Not yet.

"You, on the other hand, are the voice of reason."

"This is not about me!" I insist, trying to make him see. "This is about you. Do you know what they will want to do to you? They will make you a target. They may even begin to think it was you."

"Me?" Daniel looks at me as if I have gone mad. "What reason would I have to hurt Alice Walsh?"

"People don't need reasons!" I step closer. I am an inch away from shaking him. Shaking some sense into him. "Look at what they've done to Kate! They will come up with one and tell it to themselves until they believe it's true!"

He works up a smile. "Thanks, man, I appreciate it."

Finally, I let go of his wrist. "Why take this lightly?" I ask him. "What is wrong with you?"

"What else would you have me do?" he asks.

"Take it seriously!"

"You think I am not taking this seriously?" Daniel sits

back against his desk, still in his *Messhemd*, an alb. He looks at the stole he so carelessly threw across the chair. "This is my life! My whole life. And in a few hours, it will be no more."

"Maybe it was a shit life," I say, and think of my life, the girlfriends I've had, who stayed with me for years, whom I allowed to stay, although I always knew there was something I'd still need to figure out. Suddenly I am furious with me, for living a lie all this time. I am furious with me for preferring the lie to the truth myself, because it was more comfortable.

"No." Daniel shakes his head. "No, it wasn't." He breathes in, closes his eyes. "Maybe I wasn't strong enough for it."

And suddenly, I cannot bear that either. Does he also feel like he wasted ten years, twenty? What am I doing chastising someone for telling the truth? "What is supposed to be strong about living a life that is dishonest?" There is fervour to my voice. "How is that strong?"

Daniel looks at me. "I don't know," he says calmly. "Maybe to prove to yourself that there was a higher calling, and that you could follow it? That there was more to life than your whims? That you are a little more than a selfish bastard?"

"This is not a whim," I tell him, with all the certainty I can work up.

"The doubt shows," he replies.

"This is not a whim," I repeat more firmly. "Telling the truth is not selfish."

Daniel looks at me. "Why not?"

"Because the truth is worth fighting for."

"Not justice?" Daniel asks.

"There can be no justice without truth," I say. "How can there be justice without truth?"

"But whose truth?" he asks, glancing back at the ceiling.

"No," I say. "No, no, no. There is truth. It is true that we are here. It is true what you are feeling. It is true that Alice Walsh is dead. That we are alive. And that life is too precious to waste on lies. And if we have not found the truth yet, it is because we have not looked closely enough, we have not understood well enough, we have not asked enough people, we were too lazy, or frightened, or righteous."

"Because we did not want it," he says under his breath. "Maybe I still don't."

"But the truth doesn't care, does it?" I ask, taking an urgent step towards him.

He watches me approach. "A moment ago you were chastising me for telling the whole truth. What's it going to be?"

"Don't make the bisexual choose," I say.

It startles a laugh out of him. A real laugh. And that, in turn, makes me laugh. It is only the third time that I have said it out loud. It is the first time that the reaction was laughter, not shock or gentle comprehension.

"So you get not to be principled?" he asks, turning towards me as I inch closer. I feel stupid inching like that. Instead of just coming out and saying it. Asking him. If he wants to touch me as badly as I have been wanting to touch him.

"I am just worried," I say. "I am worried about Kate, and that is why I say stupid fucking things."

"While we're being honest?" he asks.

"Well, what can I say, you inspire me." It is supposed to come out deadpan. I am shocked to hear it sound sincere.

"Do I now?" He smiles a little. "How much, I wonder?"

"Why not try me?" I ask. This is as close as I dare come to asking the question: Do you feel what I am feeling?

He hesitates. Then: "Do you desire Kate?"

I could roll my eyes. That is what I did whenever Annette used to needle me about Kate. Whenever anyone did.

Instead, I think about it. I make myself face it. "Not in the way that anyone might think."

"Then in which way?"

It feels like I need an eternity to form every sentence. Or not to form it, but to allow myself to utter it. "I want to watch our fingers intertwine." I swallow. Give myself permission to go on. "I want to run my knuckles along her cheek when I lie next to her." Go on. "I want to listen to her breathe." Go further. "I think I want to kiss her." Even more closely. "But I think I would not want to sleep with her. I could. But it is not a… need."

I may have just ruined this. But I promised the truth. So the truth is what Daniel got.

Daniel straightens slowly. "Now I know what's special about you," he says.

"Right," I say. My breath is coming in bursts. I almost make myself laugh at how ridiculously I am behaving. How much I want this.

"It's that you say what you think." Daniel is observing me closely. "Most of the conversations I have work very differently. It feels like people are increasingly unlearning how to tell each other the truth."

"Because it fucking hurts, the truth, that's why."

"See, that." Daniel smiles, and it looks incredulous and a little dazed. "You just said that."

I smile back, completely by instinct. "You are easily pleased, Daniel."

His eyebrows shoot upwards. "Am I? Allow me to make this harder then."

For a moment, I am actually terrified. And that is because, for a moment, so is he.

"Do you desire me?" Daniel asks.

And I am still terrified. The words take too long. They take too long to leave my mouth.

The truth, I remind myself.

"Yes," I say.

He is simply looking at me. I find I can no longer look at him. Too vulnerable.

"I have never asked anyone this question," Daniel says. "Much less a man."

"Maybe we should just kiss, like real people do," I say, breathless, glancing up at his face.

His mouth twitches. "You know that's from a song, don't you?"

"I don't, and I don't give a fuck," I say.

And then he kisses me. With all the caution of someone who is still wearing an alb. And I cannot say that I care much for the caution.

I haul him in by his lapels, my fingers clutching the white fabric. He follows with all the enthusiasm my ego requires. His hands come up to hold my cheeks. And for the next minute of kissing, we keep our hands where they are, for fear of putting them in the wrong place. For fear of making a mistake. For fear of scaring the other off or scaring ourselves off.

And then suddenly this is fine, this is more than fine, this is something I have always wanted to do, and I want to do it with him, and for some completely inexplicable reason, he would also like to do it with me, me, a man who has clearly seen better days, with less of a belly and a better haircut and a beard that has seen some grooming. But fuck me if I am going to question it.

Fuck me if telling the truth isn't worth it.

We are back at Kate's house. Kate is in the bedroom, getting changed and grabbing her suitcase before we take a proper look at our handwriting samples. I am in the bathroom, the shower already running so that the water heats up properly before I step in. My limbs are shaking. I take off my sweater, then the shirt, button by button. There is the silliest grin on my face; I can see it in the mirror. It is not the sort of smile that I often see on my face. It suits the beard and the locks and the man. It even suits the red blotches still all over his chest and his throat.

I turn away from the mirror before I get embarrassed by my own happiness. I reach out a hand to test the water, which has finally run hot. Then I take off my trousers.

As I put them onto the closed toilet lid, carefully folded, I see that something is poking out of my pocket.

It is the blank slip of paper.

That wipes the smile off my face.

Alice Walsh is dead. That is the truth. She was not my child. She was not my friend. But she was struggling in a way that I have been struggling. She was alive, and now she is dead. Because someone murdered her and cut her up and left her lying in her own bed in pieces. That is the truth.

My body is still shaking, but it is for a different reason now.

I stare at the slip of paper. Then I bend over, put it onto the top of the lid and write a single sentence:

I will find out who did this to you.

Then I step into the shower. Thirty minutes later, I have shaved and dressed and brought out my own suitcase. Packed and ready, we sit down and bend over the coffee table. Kate is next to me, opening the envelope with the slips of paper.

"Ready?" she asks me.

And I am so very ready.

The truth will win out.

We have sorted the slips of paper into different categories: suspects, potentials, strangers. We will go through all of them, of course, but prioritise our suspects. After tea, consisting of oven potatoes with thyme and caramelised carrots and an alibi side of salad, I consult the list we made a few days ago. It still consists of

Megan Walsh
Patrick Walsh
Father Daniel
Sean O'Doherty
William O'Rawe

I mark everyone with a plus who owns a rifle that we know of, namely William, Sean, and Daniel. Then Kate takes the pen out of my hands and crosses out Daniel's name, throwing me a grin that is downright dirty.

She walked in on us in the sacristy. Of course she did.

Then we make another list. Of people who were close to both Kate and Alice Walsh, whom we may not think of as suspects, but whom we should make sure to check. Florence O'Rawe goes on it, so do Tessa and Elizabeth Adams. We do not have samples from Elizabeth, but Tessa actually filled out a slip of paper, without partaking in the Holy Communion. How accommodating everyone is being.

I am actually grinning as we lean over the coffee table.

Kate unfolds the note attached to the brick, straightens it out on top of the table.

"We don't have a sample from Sean, so William O'Rawe should be first," I say, reaching for it and placing it above the threatening note. And then we both lean in even closer. We stare at the words. I can feel Kate's cheek right next to me. For a moment, I remember what I told Daniel. I think I want to kiss her.

Then I focus on the letters. And we start comparing.

The handwriting is not William's.

He wrote down a children's song, the same that he had put on the wreath that I had seen at the memorial. Girls and boys come out to play, the Moon doth shine as bright as day. It may have been a song he had intended to sing to the child he had fathered. If he was the father. We still don't have proof. It may have been a song he sang to Alice Walsh when she was young. It certainly isn't his handwriting. Nor is it Patrick's. Or Megan's, or Tessa's, or Florence's.

I am no longer grinning. Instead, I am actually tearing my hair. It is the perfect length for tearing. If I am being honest with myself, I was convinced it would be William O'Rawe's handwriting. He has the means, the mindset, he could have the motive. Not just for threatening Kate, but also for murdering Alice Walsh. The children's song strikes me as suspicious, but the handwriting simply doesn't match.

Now, I am going through the samples of strangers, whose link with Kate is so tenuous that it would be a miracle if we hit a match. Patients, mostly. Next on my list would have been Sean, but we have no sample of his. I turn to Kate. "Do you have anything that could serve as a handwriting sample from Sean? Notes he left you and that you kept, letters?"

Kate does not look at me but keeps staring at the slip of paper in her hands. Her expression is tired.

"Kate?" I ask. "A shopping list? A Post-it note? Anything would do, really."

She puts down the slip of paper. Right above the threatening note. "Look at the As," she says, voice tense.

I lean in even closer.

The As.

It is as if my own frustration has been washed away in the way a pint of beer washes away all your aches after a long exhausting day at a rally. Excitement is already thrumming through me. Kate is right. The As are awfully similar.

"Who is this from?" I ask, my voice notably excited. A stranger after all, then. God, who would have thought? A patient, probably. A patient who saw her scalpel. A patient bearing a grudge, something we may not even be aware of.

Kate does not reply. All she does is turn over the slip of paper. On the back, the person has written their name in clear, clean letters.

No.

No, no, no.

"We have to be sure," I say.

"Yes," Kate says. "Let's go through them again. All of them."

I nod. All I can do is nod.

Five hours. Five hours we have spent poring over the note attached to the brick and the slips of paper collected from the congregation. We have compared letters, Os and As and Ts. We have double-checked every slip of paper. We narrowed it down to three possibilities. We took a break, ate the leftovers, cold potatoes and carrots, our fingers sticky with cold grease and caramelised sugar. We returned to it with fresh eyes. All the time, dusk was breathing down my neck, the light in the room changing, the sky turning red first through the window, then blue, grey, and finally black, just to let me know how much we are running out of time. We should be off already. Off to the hotel.

Now it is fully dark out, and the moon has already risen and set again, and we are staring at the coffee table, sitting next to each other, knees drawn up to our chests. Kate is wearing one of my soft sweaters. The phone has been ringing, but neither of us has answered. We are not looking at each other, because the moment that we do, one of us is going to have to say it, and neither of us wants to.

It is Daniel's handwriting.

This is a truth I did not want to know.

Kate speaks first. She leans into me, her head on my shoulder, and says: "I'm sorry."

I allow my head to fall against hers. The scent of her shampoo is clean and familiar and calming. Today, I stood in the sacristy and I kissed that man. The past few months, Kate has been sleeping with him. God.

"There might be an explanation," Kate says, but her voice is so pained that I know she's saying it only to comfort me. And to comfort herself.

"Oh, there will be an explanation," I say. I rise to my feet. My skin is hot with how stupid I feel. How I have been made a fool of. It is hot with anger. "And we're going to go get it."

Kate wraps a hand around my bare ankle. It makes me still. "Shouldn't we think this through?" she asks.

"No," I say, because that is the last thing I want to do. "We should go to him and find out what is going on. What else he isn't telling us."

"He cannot be the father of Alice Walsh's baby, Jan," she says quietly.

"Maybe he lied," I say. "What do we know? Maybe they slept with each other, and he lied about it."

"Wasn't there anything else in the slips of paper?" she insists. "Any other message that struck you as odd?"

I am barely holding it together when I push William O'Rawe's paper slip into her hand. "O'Rawe wrote down a children's song. He may have sung that to her when she was a kid. Or he may have intended to sing it to their child. We have no way of knowing. But we do know that Father Daniel wrote that note tied to that brick, and I want answers. I want to know why he is bothering you, and I want it to stop."

Kate is still looking at me. "Is this about me?"

"No," I admit, even though saying the truth is costing me.

"Let's call the police," she suggests, stroking my ankle. Her thumb is too gentle.

"We're just going to talk to him," I say, obstinately.

Her voice turns a little sharper. "You sound like Sean."

"Do this for me." The words break out of me. "Please."

One last stroke across my bare skin. Then Kate is on her feet. "Let me fetch a matching jacket," she says, and I find that I can take a breath and not fall apart over this. Not yet.

23:25

We step out of Kate's door. I am watching every shadow. For a man with a rifle. My hand is balled into a fist in my pocket, around two slips of treacherous paper.

I see nothing but trees and hear nothing but rustling leaves and feel nothing but the heat of my skin. The shame, the anger, the hurt. They burn so hot.

We get into the rental. Kate will be driving. I don't trust myself to.

When we approach the church, there are still quite a few cars parked outside. My hands are shaking when I open the car door. The cold air wraps me in an embrace that is not welcome. I need my blood hot for this. I know that I am soft. God, did he know? Did he take one look at me, and recognise the way I looked at him, and decide there and then that he could use me?

We go into the church. The doors are not locked. The church is cold and quiet, as cold as the night outside and even quieter, no more snow crunching under our shoes, ice crystals breaking under our soles. Just the hollow echo of our steps on the stone. He does not seem to be here.

"In the rectory, then," Kate says and starts moving towards the sacristy. "The sacristy has a connecting door."

Once we have reached the door, I reach for the handle. I pull, and it opens without effort. We step into the room; it is pitch-black, the curtains drawn in front of the only window. We make our way to the connecting door to the rectory. I am in a hurry. My brain is not being kind. It is telling me that this makes no sense. That Daniel isn't like that. That it doesn't add up, the letter that was left on the night he drove over to tell me Kate had been attacked. But maybe he is working with someone. Maybe with William O'Rawe. Maybe with Sean O'Doherty. Maybe I am wrong. Maybe I am...

Shut up, I tell my brain. Just shut up. We will confront him. We will find out why the fuck he is doing this sick shit.

We will find out what else he's done. To Kate. To Alice Walsh. To God knows who.

I push the handle down. This door, too, swings open.

We step into a low corridor, walls painted white, simple cream-coloured carpeting. There are a few prints on the wall, drawings of the local fauna, probably came with the building.

I am still fumbling for a light switch when I hear steps.

Suddenly the lights are turned on.

Daniel is coming towards us from the other end of the corridor. My first thought is to charge.

Then I realise what that expression on his face is.

Terror.

"Lock the door!" he calls out.

Kate is turning to obey, but I stop her with a hand on her arm. He may be trying to trap us.

"Do it!" Daniel says, his voice desperate. "They're coming!"

He has reached us, reaches between us to lock the door to the sacristy. He looks pale and frightened and his fingers are shaking. "I don't, I can't…"

He turns around and rushes back through the corridor. Kate is one step ahead of me as we rush to follow him to the front room, but I am right behind her.

That is why I barely manage to avoid crashing into her when she stops so suddenly. I reach for her shoulders to steady myself. My chest against her back, her hair in my nose. I can hear her breath. The sharp intake. The sound of shock and the smell of fear.

We have a clear view of the front door of the rectory from here. Of the windows to both sides.

A clear view of the silhouettes.

They are all standing outside around the front door of the rectory. Six of them. Six silent silhouettes.

Every single one of them is holding a rifle.

EVIDENCE #10603
CATEGORY: NOTICE
DESCRIPTION:
A POSTER PUT UP BY NEIGHBOURHOOD PROTECTION WITH ADDED WRITING AT THE BOTTOM, FOUND OUTSIDE ANNACAIRN CHURCH.

NEIGHBOURHOOD PROTECTION

PROTECT YOUR NEIGHBOURHOOD
At Neighbourhood Protection we believe in partnership between the local communities and the police (Policing and Community Safety Partnerships (PCSPs)). We help you protect YOURSELF, we help you protect YOUR property, we help reduce YOUR fear of crime in YOUR community.

FIND OUT MORE...
Sean O'Doherty, Rostrevor Rd
Sodsodsod67@hotmail.com

PROTECT OUR NEIGHBOURHOOD!

PROTECT OUR WOMEN!!

We won't stand for this!!
We won't let them poison our teenagers
We won't let them fuck our women
We won't let them come in here and beat up our men
We won't let them abort our children
WE WON'T STAND FOR THIS
THIS IS OUR LAND
OUR WOMEN
OUR CHILDREN
OURS!!!!!!!!!!!!

Day 6

MONDAY 7TH JANUARY 2019

EVIDENCE #10613

CATEGORY: TEXT MESSAGES

DESCRIPTION:

A SEQUENCE OF TEXT MESSAGES LEFT ON THE PHONE OF ALICE
WALSH, SHORTLY BEFORE HER DEATH; THEY WERE SENT VIA A
PROVIDER FOR ANONYMOUS TEXT MESSAGING AND CANNOT BE
TRACKED BACK TO THE SENDER.

#1
Hi Ally

#2
Sorry, I know you don't like these texts. But it's
important we do this so that this stays between us. I
know you don't want your parents to know, and that
just makes sense.

#3
You messaged me and you said you needed to tell
me something. You said to come by during my lunch
break. You made me nervous. Can you believe it?
You, making me nervous. Just like that.

#4
I'm coming over right now.

#5
I can't wait. I can't wait to see you. I love you.
I love you very much.

There is no light except the pale stars in the sky, and no sound except our laboured breathing. We are standing in the dark front room, all three of us staring out at the silhouettes.

The silhouettes holding their rifles. Not just one, but six of them.

They are so close. If any of them is a practised shooter, I have no doubt that they will not miss their mark.

"Step back," I whisper. "Slowly."

"What do we do?" Kate asks.

"The police," I say. "Use your mobile, Kate."

"No signal," Daniel says. "There's no signal here."

"Landline," I hiss.

The ensuing silence tells me all I need to know.

Daniel does not have a landline.

Fuck.

Fuck, fuck, fuck.

I take a careful step back, but I am hesitant. I want to know who they are. I want to confront them. Hell, I want to confront Daniel.

"They will go away," I say. "All doors are locked? All windows?"

"Yes," Daniel says quietly.

I turn to face him. "Then perhaps you'd like to explain yourself."

He opens his mouth and closes it. It is impossible to read

his expression in the dark. He lifts his arm, perhaps to reach for me. I take a measured step back.

"There are six people with rifles outside my house, and I'm scared?" he tries. His voice is tense. From the corner of my eye, I see that Kate is slowly inching towards me. I move in her direction, to make sure she does not inadvertently come any closer to the window.

"Do you recognise this?" I ask, reaching into my pocket to pull out the slip of paper he filled out for Alice.

His brow furrows as he takes it off me. "It's pretty dark," he says. "But I think it's one of your slips of paper, from the service…"

He looks up suddenly. His voice is tinged with an emotion I cannot name. "Did you find him? The culprit?"

I breathe out through the nose. Breathe in. Stay calm. "Yes," I say. "It's you."

Silence.

Then Daniel speaks. "You can't be serious."

I take one step towards him, and we are face to face. Only inches separating us. It is so different from the last time we stood like this. Bile is working its way up my throat. My eyes are burning all of the sudden.

"You cannot be serious," I hiss.

"You can't believe that it was me, I...!" he says, but I do not let him go on. I thrust the second piece of paper into his hands, the note that was attached to the brick.

"Then tell me what this is! Tell me why it has your handwriting on it!"

Our fingers brush as he takes it from me. A shiver runs through my treacherous body. Breathing heavily, I refuse to step back. Fuck. My blood is thrumming again. I cannot fight the six people outside, the six huntsmen and their glinting rifles. But I can fight this one man.

He looks at it. Holds it up into the little light that is filtering in through the window. When he speaks again, his voice is quiet. "It's one of my Post-its. The notes I use for my sermon. Where did you get this?"

"It was tied to a brick that was used to smash the window in Kate's bedroom," I say through clenched teeth.

"What?" If Daniel is faking his shock, he is faking it well.

"Could someone have picked it up from your desk?" Kate asks. "Who has access to the sacristy?"

Daniel looks miserable. "Me," he says. "I'm the only one with a key. But I don't always lock the door."

He is trying to move away, but my arm shoots forward, my fingers clamp around his wrist. "If you are seriously telling me it wasn't you who tied that note to that brick and put that brick through the window, it must be someone who has regular access. There have been so many letters." I get even closer, because I am desperate. "Better make this count, Daniel."

"Listen, I wish I could explain it!" he says. "But I don't, I just know... Why would I want to threaten Kate? It makes no sense!"

He stares at me. We are so close. I can feel his breath on my lips.

That is when we hear it.

That is the unmistakable sound of a fist crashing against the door.

I whirl around. "Get down!" I hiss. Through the window, I catch a glimpse of the silhouettes. Five. There are only five of them left.

The fist crashes against the door again. And again. And again.

Then silence.

And then we hear the voice.

"Come out."

Behind me, Daniel recoils. Whoever is standing in front of the door, they are calling out to us.

"Come out."

The voices. Now it is all of them, speaking at the same time. Whispering.

"Come out."

It is impossible to recognise them, to tell them apart. All I can hear are the words.

"Come out."

Kate comes up to my side, planting her feet. I turn back to Daniel, my heart in my throat. God, all I want is the truth. "You claim someone has taken the notes from your desk. And yet you say you are the only one with a key. Now is the time to do better, Daniel."

His eyes are wide with fear. "They may have bulk stolen them, what do I..."

But then he stops himself.

And that is when I allow myself to hope. Because he looks like he might be able to offer us another suspect.

"Tessa," he says.

"Come out."

Kate draws in a sharp breath. "Tessa Adams? Our bus driver?"

"She has a key. For the cleaning."

"Tessa," I repeat, incredulous.

"Come out."

"Why are you shaking your head?" Daniel asks. "Are you seriously telling me you believe it's me throwing bricks at you rather than Tessa Adams? I did not throw that brick through your window, Kate. I did not write you threatening letters!"

All I hear for a moment is her breathing.

"I believe you," Kate finally says.

"Come out."

Her hand lifts, and she touches his hand with hers. I watch their fingers intertwine.

"Does Tessa Adams have a reason to threaten Kate?" I ask.

"Come out."

"No," Kate says, turning to me. "But her brother might."

"William," Daniel mutters.

We all of us turn back to the window.

There they stand. The huntsmen and their rifles.

"Come out."

Daniel may not have convinced me yet, but there is one thing I am convinced of: one of those huntsmen is William O'Rawe.

And another is Sean O'Doherty.

"Come out."

"What do we do?" Kate asks.

"Come out!"

I'm still staring at the silhouettes, trying not to feel so bloody helpless. My hand seeks Kate's and finds it. Our fingers intertwine.

Come out.

00:51

Come out.

Clouds collect in the sky, obliterating the stars. The last light in which we could see.

They are still there.

Still whispering.

Come out.

My eyes are burning. I am pacing to keep awake, but my vision keeps blurring. Kate is on my right, Daniel on my left.

"Are there only five of them now?" he asks, quietly, voice blurry with tiredness. I glance out of the window. He's right. I only count five of them, and no one has been knocking against the door for a while. "Or is the last one still standing in front of the door? They have to leave at some point, don't they?" he asks, and his voice breaks on the words.

My hand finds his.

"Did you tell them anything else?" I ask. "Have you spoken to anyone since the service?"

He hesitates.

"Megan Walsh called."

"What did you tell her? Daniel, what did you tell her?"

Daniel breathes out. "Everything. I told her everything."

I am growing increasingly desperate. "That you encouraged Alice Walsh to have an abortion? That she outed herself to you?"

His voice is small when he replies. "I had to confess."

I turn back to the silhouettes.

There will be no absolution from them.

Come out.

Come out.

Come out!

What was that?
Who's there?

I start back into consciousness.

Disoriented, I look around. The rectory. The huntsmen. The huntsmen and their rifles!

I jump to my feet. Then I sink right back down. A spell of dizziness. Slowly, laboriously, I work myself back up. Onto all fours, and isn't that demeaning. I stagger towards the window and peek through the sheer curtains.

The silhouettes are gone.

They are gone.

Where are they?

Why am I alone?

Where are Daniel and Kate?

Why is no one whispering?

Come out.

What is that sticky liquid running down my neck?

I lift my hand. Even before I have touched it, I know that I am bleeding. That that is blood soaking the wool of my sweater.

Fighting a wave of nausea, I lift my shaking hands, try to trace the wound. From the way it is shaped, the way my head hurts, I think someone must have hit me from behind. Someone must have sneaked up on us from behind.

From the church.

They must have taken Daniel and Kate.

Still battling the nausea, I struggle to my feet. Supporting myself against the wall, I stagger towards the corridor leading to the sacristy, smearing the wallpaper with blood as I go. The moment I reach the corridor and hit the light switch, I see that the door to the sacristy has been broken down.

My vision blurs. I stagger into the church. Its doors have been thrown wide open. It is dark in here, and dark outside. The cold wind is howling under the arches. There are wet footprints on the floor. They lead outside into the cold, dark night.

I follow them.

Once outside, I spare a moment to be grateful that it is winter, and that there is snow on the ground. The tracks of many trampling boots are impossible to miss, even with blurry vision and a splitting headache and spells of nausea hitting me sideways, bile crawling up my throat. I swallow it down as I make to follow the tracks. I try and run. My vision tilts, my feet drag. I shake my head. My vision clears a little. Bile. I swallow. Blurry. Shake my head. Bile. Swallow. Blurry. Shake.

I keep stumbling through the snow as quickly as I am able, fumbling for my phone. I watch the screen, pleading with the phone to pick up a signal as I struggle away from the church, following the tracks. They are leading into the graveyard. The ground is slippery.

The moment I've thought it, I fall. My hands hit the ground. The snow is cold and harsh and hard, glazed with ice. I suppress the noise of pain with all the strength I have. Cannot give myself away. Running out of time. I struggle back onto my feet. Drag my body along the tracks. My knees, threatening to give out. My feet, threatening to cave in. If I take one close look at them, they will cave, break apart, the metatarsal bones cracking first, breaking my soles in two. There is still blood running down my neck, sticky on my skin, red on my hands.

Voices.

There are voices.

I drag my eyes up from my feet.

Silhouettes. Up in the graveyard. Up on the hill. By Alice Walsh's memorial. One of them is speaking. I cannot make out the words. And there is something. Something dangling from the thickest branch of the yew tree.

It is a noose.

All the graveyard candles surrounding Alice Walsh's memorial are burning. Their red glow lights up the silhouettes, throwing stark shadows across their bodies, their faces, the gnarled boughs of the yew tree twisting and winding their way up into the night. Kate and Daniel are kneeling in the snow on the ground right below the noose. It is tied from thick pale rope. There is blood on Kate's face. Daniel is kneeling doubled over, as if someone has hit him so hard that he cannot breathe.

The noose is laid around his neck.

They are surrounded by six silhouettes, and now there is finally enough light to recognise them: Megan Walsh. Sean O'Doherty. William O'Rawe. Patrick Walsh. Florence O'Rawe.

All of them. Every single one of those we had on our list.

And then there is the sixth. I recognise the wellies and the cardigan before I recognise her.

Tessa Adams.

She warned me. I cannot say that she didn't warn me. There they all stand. Under the noose. Sean is bent over Daniel and Kate, black cloth sacks in his hand. He reaches for Daniel first. Daniel twists and twists and turns, but Sean grips his hair and yanks his head back with such force that a scream is ripped from Daniel's throat. Sean pushes the bag over Daniel's head, fastens it, then turns to Kate. Even from this distance I can see her eyes, as bright as stars. She spits

269

on the ground in front of him, spewing out blood and saliva. He grabs her chin, forces her head up.

Then he spits in her face. He pulls the bag over her head, fastens it, then steps back.

Bile. Rising. Bile. Swallow. I cannot bear the sight, Kate's and Daniel's heads swallowed up by the dark cloth as if they had no faces. Blurry. Shake. Swallow. I crouch down behind a headstone for a fallen soldier. Above me, one of the branches of the yew tree is twisting and winding and reaching into the night, twisting like the body of a tortured beast. I cling to the cold rough stone to keep upright. I am close enough to understand what they are saying. At first, I do not recognise the voice that is speaking. It is so soft. I expect it to be William's, or Sean's. Or even Megan's.

But it isn't.

It takes me three painful, breathless moments to realise that it is Patrick who is speaking. Patrick Walsh, his soft voice no longer shy, ringing out across the graveyard: "You're ready then."

Kate tries to speak through cloth. Of Daniel, all I hear is his laboured breath. "Patrick," she says, her voice cruelly muffled. She is turning her head, disoriented, her tone desperate. Short of breath. "I have done nothing to Alice. Not Daniel, not me. We did nothing to her."

"Nothing?" Patrick's voice is pained. "That's what you think?"

"We did not kill her," Kate says, her voice so dull and broken-hearted. "We did not murder your daughter, Patrick."

"But you murdered the child in her body."

I can feel my body go still. Utterly, utterly still. So does Kate. The shock hits us both. It is draining me of every thought, every sentiment, everything but the dawning, the horrible realisation.

Patrick knew. He knew. The man who dragged his wife back from the airport, seventeen years ago, refusing her the choice. He knew that his daughter was pregnant. He knew that she had aborted. He knew that Kate helped her.

"Did you think I didn't know?" Patrick asks, and there may be tears in his eyes from the way his voice sounds. The tears of a desperate man. The branches of the yew tree seem to be moving in the red glow of the candles. Seem to be reaching for Daniel. For Kate. For me. It feels as if they are wrapping around my throat. I cannot breathe. Cannot breathe. We never thought of him. Never suspected him, just because he cried a little. "Alice always was a daddy's girl. She may have kept it from her mother, but she couldn't keep it from me. I wouldn't tell the police, I wouldn't disgrace my own child like that, but she didn't keep it from me. She told me after she'd killed the baby."

"Then you know that I didn't do anything," Kate says. She is struggling to draw enough air into her lungs through the cloth. "You know that she ordered the pills. That she took them."

"You told her!"

And suddenly, Patrick is shouting. "That was my grandchild growing in my daughter's body, and you told her how to murder it!"

I rise. My vision tilts. The flickering candles dance in front of my eyes, red and red and red. The yew tree seems to be growing larger, reaching up into the sky to blot out the stars with its thick branches. The thick noose. I sink back to the ground, dropping my phone as I desperately try to hold on.

My phone.

I glance at the screen.

There is one bar on the screen. One single bar.

I have a signal.

"It was her choice, Patrick." Daniel speaks up. Laboriously. His voice is unrecognisable through the cloth tied over his head, the rough fabric scratching his mouth. "Alice chose to do it."

"She should not have been given that choice!" Snot is running from Patrick's nose. He is crying in earnest now. The silhouettes draw their circle closer while I punch in the three numbers. 999.

"That wasn't up to you, Patrick," Daniel says.

It takes Patrick Walsh two steps, then he is in front of Daniel. Two seconds, then the butt of his rifle comes down on Daniel's head. It is so vicious a blow that I can barely suppress a noise of pain myself, my hands scrambling for purchase on the headstone, the stone leaving bloody scratches on my palm.

Then a click. There is a voice on the other end of the line, asking me where I am. Daniel lets out another shout, falls to the ground. I flinch, nearly drop the phone. As hushed as I can, I try to speak into the phone. The words will not come out at first. The blood loss, the nausea, the trembling. Eight words, I manage eight of them: graveyard Annacairn six armed men life and death. Kate makes to move towards

Daniel, but she does not know where to go, and Sean is next to her in a moment, restraining her. "Don't worry, Pat, I've got her."

Patrick barely seems to be listening. I can barely make out his words through his sobs. Can barely understand the voice at the other end of the line anymore, asking me more questions. "Who's it up to, then?" Patrick asks. "I'm her father. Her father!"

"It was her choice!" Kate spits out, still struggling. My vision tilts. There is a ringing in my ear. When I look back at the screen, I see that the call has been cut off. I can only pray that they are on their way. Sean attempts to put a hand over Kate's mouth, but she keeps fighting, keeps speaking for as long as she can: "Dying, that was not her choice! She was murdered! Why aren't you out for her murderer? What are you doing with Daniel and—"

Sean's hand clamps down. The sounds of her furious words, trying to claw their way out, fill the night like helplessly flailing beasts brought to slaughter, just like the noises Daniel makes, noises of pain and fighting to stay conscious holding on on on while my hands slip on the stone. I have to do something. I have to. I have to…

"You encouraged her," Patrick says, his voice raw from the tears. "You were supposed to guide her, both of you. You, Father Daniel, you were her priest. Instead, you told her it was all right. You told her there could be absolution."

The butt of his rifle is still raised above Daniel's head. Gently, Patrick lowers it to touch Daniel's forehead through the hood. Almost as if he was caressing it. It startles a shaky groan out of Daniel. His head is swaying from the right to the left. He is swaying, struggling even to rise back to his hands and knees, while Patrick continues speaking. His voice barely makes it above a whisper. "There can be no absolution for you."

Patrick kneels then. Kneels down before Daniel's trembling body, his trembling arms and legs and hands. Patrick reaches out with one hand. Pulls up Daniel's swaying head by the chin. Reaches for the noose. He begins to pull. Pulling the rope tighter. "No absolution for any of us."

He is still pulling. Still pulling it tighter. Even as I struggle to my feet, I do not know what it is that I can do to save them.

And then I do.

A desperate bid, but it might just work.

I have to tell the truth.

"Patrick! Megan!"

Everyone except Patrick turns around to face me. Above me, the wood of the yew creaks. Crackles. As if it was laughing at me. Sean is the first to react. He trains his weapon on me with relish. So does William O'Rawe. Only Megan Walsh's expression is impassive. There are no tears in her eyes. There is nothing. I wonder if she is really here with us. Tessa Adams's expression is unmoving, too. Only Florence O'Rawe draws in a panicked breath.

I swallow down the bile. A weak link. Good. Because none of the others seem to have any compunctions about shooting me. The truth is whispering to me. I can hear it. Can hear it say: you can rely on me.

If only I knew what the truth was. If only I knew for

sure. I take two staggering steps towards them. Then I come to a halt, both hands raised, because I think my knees will give out if I do not stop. "Patrick, you have the wrong man."

Patrick does not even tilt his head in my direction.

"Been waiting for you to show up," Sean says, looking me up and down with all the despicable fear and the fearful disgust that this young man bears for bodies turning old and frail und unreliable, reminding him of what awaits in his own future. I almost smile. It is coming for you, too, Sean, I would like to tell him. Frailty and death is waiting for all of us.

"You're angry with the wrong man, Patrick," I continue, my voice as weak as my body. "You're looking for someone to blame, but you aren't looking in the right place."

And Patrick—

Patrick is shifting.

I know that this is critical. I cannot be the one who tells him that his daughter slept with a close friend; he will simply deny it if he hears it from me. So instead, I say: "You have been lied to, Patrick."

"My daughter did not lie to me," Patrick says, hand still lying on the thick noose around Daniel's throat. "She told me about their conversations. And he admitted it in front of his entire congregation. He admitted it again, to my wife, on the phone today."

I shake my head. "I was not referring to Father Daniel. He did not lie to you."

"Then who?" Patrick is turning towards me, away from Daniel. Everyone is. I have their attention. God,

275

thank you. I swallow. Blurry. Bile. Keep swallowing. Keep speaking.

"It isn't my secret to tell," I say, pretending to be calm. Extremely calm, even while my heart is racing and my vision is blurring and I can feel my knees growing weaker and weaker as if I am about to snap in half. While I can hear the yew cackling at me, can feel its arms and branches and twigs reaching for me with thick sharp fingers, ready to pull me up by the throat and strangle me alive, ready to cut my skin and watch me bleed out on the ground.

Because I have no idea. I have no idea whether it was William O'Rawe or Sean O'Doherty or another friend of Patrick's altogether, and I will only have one shot at this.

I cannot be sure.

I have no way of being sure.

So I take a leap: "I think you should come clean, William."

Everyone turns to William O'Rawe.

He shakes his head. Incredulous. "Pat, what's he on about?"

I swallow. I may be wrong, but I think—

I think his voice is shaking.

"Florence, you didn't know, am I right?" I ask. Even in the dark, I can see her staring at me with wide brown eyes.

"Or did you?" I ask gently. Gently now. I take another step. The truth is propping me up. Raising my back. My body. "It's all right. It helps, saying it out loud. It feels better, not having to hide anything anymore."

"Why are we letting him speak?" William hisses.

Florence's face is flying this way and that as she tries to look both at him and me at the same time.

"What is she not supposed to say a word about, Will?" Megan asks.

And God, she sounds so tired.

So tired as she lifts her rifle and aims it at the man standing next to her.

She is aiming it at William O'Rawe.

Tessa moves towards Megan, but William shakes his head wildly, motioning for her to stay put. Kate is sitting up. Daniel is still on all fours, attempting to catch his breath. All that can be heard for a moment is the violent trembling of Daniel's body in the snow and the silence of a question that goes unanswered.

"Come on," Megan says. The yew tree is bending over her. "Out with it."

"Megan, point that rifle somewhere else," Tessa Adams growls.

"There's nothing to come out with," William says.

"You know that that isn't true, William," I say, inching closer. Florence has lowered her rifle. William's aim is wavering. Patrick has turned away from Daniel and Kate. It is only Sean now who still has his weapon trained on the two of them. My voice grows firmer. "There are witnesses, William. In the plural. They are prepared to come forward and tell the police what you and Alice Walsh were involved in."

"There was nothing that Alice and I were involved in!" he says even as Tessa hisses at me: "Shut up!"

277

But William is shifting. Shifting. Nervously eyeing the barrel pointed right at him.

Megan turns to me. Her eyes still look as dark and violent as they did in the bright light of her kitchen. "You were kind enough, Mr Loose, in my kitchen, even if you didn't listen. Now do me another kindness and tell me."

"It's going to hurt," I tell her softly, and I mean it.

She does not move a muscle.

I take a deep breath. Then I say it. I tell the truth. I don't embellish it, I don't add to it, I don't subtract, I do not wine it, dine it, take it to bed. I just tell it: "Alice was sleeping with a friend of her father's. This man was the father of her child. She intended to tell that man about the abortion, if after the fact."

The silence is complete.

And I can feel the truth smile gently at the back of my mind.

Patrick lowers his rifle. "No," he whispers, while Megan Walsh straightens.

"Was it you?" she asks William. Her voice is as cold as can be.

William opens his mouth. He glances at Florence. He glances at his sister.

"No," she says, fiercely.

And that is when we hear it.

The distant sound of a siren.

Finally, William looks back at Patrick and Megan.

He shakes his head.

Tessa lets out a relieved breath. Megan closes her eyes, begins to lower her weapon. William smiles a watery smile at Patrick Walsh. The corner of Patrick's mouth twitches upwards, at least.

And perhaps I was wrong. Perhaps it was Sean O'Doherty. Perhaps it was neither of them. Perhaps it was a friend of Patrick's that I don't know.

It doesn't matter as long as I get Kate and Daniel out of here.

I take a step towards them as William approaches Patrick, slapping a hand onto his shoulder.

"Then where did you go?"

It is Florence. Florence who has suddenly spoken up. Who has realised that finally, when she trains a rifle on her husband, he will have to answer her. "Where was it that you always went off to, these past few months? How did you know that someone had hit Kate O'Leary in the graveyard, Will?"

He shakes his head. "It has nothing to do—"

"Just tell me," she says, desperation tinging her voice. "Just tell me where you went. Tell us where you went. Tell us where you went if it wasn't to Alice." Her voice is rising and rising. "Tell me the truth! Just, finally, tell me the truth!"

He is still looking at her. And then his expression twists, and tears are in his eyes, and they are running down his cheeks. "You know I've always wanted a child, Flory. You know."

Now Florence is crying, too. She says nothing.

William turns to Megan and Patrick. "You know I always did. Pat, you know. She wanted it. She told me she wanted it."

Everyone knows that he is not talking about Florence.

He is talking about Alice.

The relief is so great, and it hits me so unexpectedly, that my knees finally buckle. I sink to the ground. I thought he would deny it. I was certain he would. I did not think I would win. That the truth would win out.

Just like that.

My vision is no longer tilting. Just gently swaying. Swaying towards the ground. Towards blessed oblivion. The siren is growing louder.

"Did you kill her?" Megan Walsh asks. So tired. She sounds as tired as I am feeling. Drained.

I force myself to look up at William once more. Watch him look at Patrick. "She aborted my child," he says, voice a mess, face a mess, tears and snot and blood. "You wouldn't have let that happen, Pat. Back when it was Megan, you didn't allow that to happen, and I failed."

He doesn't deny it.

I try to struggle back to my feet. One last time. Someone has to help Kate and Daniel back onto their feet. Someone has to explain it all to the police once they arrive. It must be them, this siren I'm hearing.

"I couldn't prevent it, Pat," William continues. "Not like you could, back then. I'm sorry. So sorry, Pat."

The sirens are here now. They're here. And I am on my feet.

That is why I see it.

How Megan Walsh lifts her rifle.

I do not even have time to shout.

She shoots William where he stands.

I am on my feet and hurtling my body towards her. Megan raises her rifle and aims it at me. William's body is still on its way to the ground.

02:59:51

William's body hits the ground. I freeze, raise my arms. Megan is staring at me.

"Please," I say. Bile. Fear. The yew, grabbing me. Its sharp sharp branches cutting my throat. "Stop here. It won't bring her back."

"Nothing can bring her back," she says.

02:59:59

From the corner of my eye, I catch sight of a movement. Another rifle, rising.

Taking aim.

The shot resounds through the graveyard.

03:00:00

Megan Walsh is dead.

It was a perfect shot. It was Tessa Adams, and she fired a perfect shot.

"For fuck's sake!" Sean is shouting. He is moving quickly, a true professional, disarming Tessa. Tessa is trying to get to William. She is shouting his name. Shouting for her twin. He is dead. Megan's body is still moving. Still convulsing. I don't know where to look. My vision is growing black. Blood is running warm and wet down the back of my head. Running and running. My vision.

Kate.

Daniel.

I stagger towards them. Maybe I'm crawling. Maybe that's why my hands are cold as ice. Why my clothes are drenched. Why I'm trembling all over, my teeth chattering.

But Sean is disarming Tessa. Sean has thrown his weapon away, and he is holding her down, and then he is holding down Patrick, too. And there is the siren. The siren. It's so close now. So very close. Then there are steps, many many many steps coming up the hill. I can hear them. I can hear the shouts and the careful orders and the sound of firearms cocking. And then black figures come running past me. Black ghosts in the graveyard. They are swarming across the white snow, surrounding the old yew tree. The old yew tree, bent and gnarled, soaking up the blood, Megan's and William's and mine, running red and thick into the snow, feeding the tree in the night under the silver light of the stars, feeding the roots, feeding and feeding the ancient roots.

As I crawl towards Kate, I can feel the roots under my hands and knees. I can feel them trembling with pleasure as they drink up our blood. Can feel them grow thick. Can feel them pulse.

My vision is growing darker and darker. I'm so close to Kate. I reach for her ankle. Her bare bloodstained ankle.

Someone presses me to the ground from above. Someone is shouting. One of the ghosts has come.

I cross my arms behind my head. I try to kneel, but the moment I do, I finally

finally

lose consciousness.

When I come to again, everything is white. The ceiling, the lights, the walls, the sheets. And the snow, falling gently from the sky outside the window in the pale grey light of dawn. Even the smell of disinfectant somehow feels white.

I glance at the alarm clock on the bedside table.

Half past four is about as dreadful a time to be in a hospital as midnight.

I sit up. I feel fine. Possibly because I have been shot up to the brim with painkillers, but if I don't ask too many questions, I'm sure that no one else will, so far be it from me to complain. Besides, there's only one question I care about.

Where are Kate and Daniel?

"Good morning. No, don't start, I didn't mean to startle you."

I start and look to my left. Detective Inspector Adam Kwiatkowski is sitting in a chair by the wall. The last time I saw him, at Ardmore Station, he took note of our complaint about the threatening letters. He looked perfectly destroyed even then, but that is nothing compared to his appearance right now. He's holding the largest cup of takeaway coffee I have ever seen. It seems to be empty, and he to be fervently mourning that fact.

Most of all, he looks horribly, horribly tired.

"Detective," I say. "Thanks for coming to our aid so quickly."

He stares at me as if I had gone mad. "Before any more people could be shot dead, you mean?"

I swallow. He puts down the massive cup, placing it onto the floor. I have just now realised that it's one of those reusable ones. Made of bamboo, I think. Floral pattern. It looks like it might have been a gift from his children.

"Detective," I manage to ask, my voice shaky even in my own ears, "where are Kate and Father Daniel?"

"They're here. Their condition is stable. I'm sorry, I should have told you that. You're the strongest of the three of you, though, so the doctors said I could ask you a few questions. That all right with you?"

"Of course," I say.

But no questions are forthcoming. He just looks at me. Then he sits up. "Let me start though by saying something. Let me say that I'm sorry we didn't properly protect you and Ms O'Leary."

I do him the favour of returning his frankness. "You didn't exactly take her seriously, I think."

He leans back. Drops his head against the wall. "I should have."

There is no absolution I can give him. "Yes," I say. "You should have."

He closes his eyes. "Can you tell me what happened last night?"

And I tell him. I tell him everything. Tell him of the threats, the handwriting samples, of the six huntsmen and the noose and William O'Rawe's final words. I tell him everything, and by the end of it, I feel exhausted. The truth is exhausting.

"William O'Rawe," the detective says, staring off into the distance. His suit is so crumpled, his shirt so wrinkled, the bags under his eyes so deep. "We had our sights on him. In fact, we were on our way to arrest him. That's the only reason why we could react so quickly to your call. We were already on our way. He left Alice Walsh an audio message before her death from a burn phone, delivering a motive as clearly as you could. Tonight was when we could tie it to him, soundly enough for a warrant of arrest. Still, without a confession…" He sighs. "A confession we won't be able to get now. Tessa Adams, though. What a family. But at least we have her in custody. Maybe she knew something. Maybe her brother told her something."

He scrubs a hand across his face. "We were on the lookout from the start for the father of the child she chose to abort. It usually is a lover or ex-lover, when the victim is a woman, or a close family member, you know. And yet…" He drops his hands. Looks at me. "Something struck me as out of the ordinary with this case. The way she was cut up. It seemed like such a statement. A message. A legacy, almost. Like someone who wished to leave something behind. It was so calculated. It didn't seem like a crime of passion."

"We thought the same thing at some point," I said. "The way her body was left, we thought the killer must have struck before, or have a very deliberate message to send. Kate looked for similar cases, but she only chanced upon one other case where the body of the victim had been treated in a similar fashion. It was here in the area, too. But the culprit has been dead for years."

The detective nods. "Oh yes, the Ryan case. We did the same thing, of course, but we couldn't come up with anything more, either. It kept troubling me, how similarly the bodies of the victims had been treated. I saw photos of Emily Ryan. The victim back then. Almost seemed to me as if someone had reconstructed her position for Alice Walsh from memory. It had me so worried, I triple-checked that her murderer was actually dead. I wanted to look into it further, but my partner and I decided we had better leads."

"Turns out you were right," I say.

He shrugs. "In the end, I'm still not sure. O'Rawe must have seen those pictures somewhere. Or it must be the wildest coincidence. Maybe Tessa Adams can tell us. I like to understand these things. Make sure there isn't anything that's been overlooked." He furrows his brow. There seems to be something more he wants to say. Then he shakes his head. "No," he mumbles. "Anyway, I will be needing a formal statement. Can you come to the station tomorrow? Then I won't have to subject you to any more questions tonight."

"Sure," I say as he rises to his feet. "I'll come by."

"Whenever suits you," he says. "Get some rest. You're safe here. And Ms O'Leary, too. You're all safe now."

05:30

I can't sleep. Keep tossing and turning. The smell of disinfectant is strong. My mind is whirring.

06:15

There are noises outside. Footsteps in the corridor.
Shuffling.
I'm frightened.

06:30

It was just the nurse preparing breakfast. Potato bread. I smile at my plate. God, I've become paranoid. No surprise, though.

After breakfast, I lie down to try and catch a couple more hours of sleep.

06:44

My brain cannot seem to calm. As if a voice was whispering to me. As if I'd forgotten something, only I can't remember what.

I need to go home and sleep in a proper bed.

It's dawn by the time I make it home.

They wouldn't let me see Kate. Or Daniel. Then the doctor on duty told me she recommended I stay another night. I told her that all I wanted was to sleep in a room that didn't smell of disinfectant, and that I was very grateful for their pains.

The doctor sighed. It had been a long night shift for her, too. She let me go.

Now I'm at Kate's house. I'll go and see her in a couple of hours. For now, I open the front door. For now, I step over the threshold. For now, I stand in the hall and breathe.

Just breathe.

Slowly, I take off my shoes. Then I make my way into the bedroom. The window, still broken. I walk to the closet and take out a fresh set of clothes. Piece by piece, I put myself back together: underwear, undershirt, sock, sock, trousers, T-shirt, sweater, cardigan. Then I take the bloody clothes from last night and put them into the washing machine. You're safe, I tell myself.

Then why are my fingers shaking?

There is something gnawing at the back of my head. As if the thin branches of the rowan tree have reached through the walls, growing straight into the house and through my skin and skull into my brain.

A legacy. That's what the Detective Inspector said. It felt as if the murderer wanted to leave a legacy. That is how I felt about it, too. I felt like this had been the work of someone who had something to say.

I sink back onto my heels in front of the washing machine and press my forehead against the smooth glass of its window.

And there is one thing I don't yet understand.

Who was the man with the rifle at Kate's house? Was it William O'Rawe? Did he have his sister Tessa steal notes from Daniel's desk to deliver them as threatening letters to us? First he kills the woman he impregnated, the moment he learns of the abortion, a crime of passion. And then he goes and mounts such a well-planned, coldly executed scheme of intimidation against Kate? Carefully collects threatening Bible quotations? The campaign against Kate was so deliberate. The murder seemed so spontaneous.

I rise to my feet. It is so quiet in the house. Dawn is spilling into the night. The light is turning grey. Everything is disappearing into white. White snow on the ground, a white sky above, the pale outline of trees as insubstantial as the fabric of a dream.

The hairs at the back of my neck are standing up.

Was it William O'Rawe I saw out there in the night? Was it a man of sixty years who ran from me that night, ran away and out onto the moor?

A noise.

It came from the sitting room.

I stand and I wait and I listen.

All I hear is the rumbling of the washing machine.

I move towards the sitting room. Past the back door.

Something rustles under my feet.

I look down.

It is a letter.

There is that whisper at the back of my head. It's the voice of truth, telling us that I am not quite there yet. Not quite. Whispering that I have not quite found out yet. Not yet.

Whispering that I am about to.

Why did they take Kate and Daniel from the rectory, but not me? If they didn't care about me, then who did? Who cared enough to throw a brick through our window, threatening the foreigner who was staying at Kate's house?

Who left this letter?

And whose breath is it that I can hear on the other side of the wall?

I push open the door to the sitting room.

There is someone sitting in the old armchair, their back turned to me. A curl of smoke is emerging from the chair.

"That is a beautiful tree outside. Did you know that there are more yew trees in Britain than in any other country? They are particularly numerous in England, of course."

I circle the armchair. When I finally see who is sitting in it, I find that it is someone who has never been on any of our lists. It isn't Patrick Walsh, it isn't Sean O'Doherty, it isn't Tessa Adams or Florence or Daniel.

Instead, I'm looking at Elizabeth Adams.

Elizabeth Adams is wearing her Sunday clothes. An emerald skirt and jacket and hat, sheer black tights, practical black shoes. She looks a little like I imagine the Queen dresses for church. Except that I have never seen the Queen smoke.

She smiles faintly but doesn't look at me. She is staring out the kitchen window at the broad boughs of the yew tree.

"Did you know that there are almost one thousand ancient yews in England and Wales? They are older than five hundred years. Some may be as old as two thousand years, or even five thousand." She looks out with a gentle expression, pulling in another gentle drag. "You have an excellent view of it from this armchair."

She seems not at all perturbed by my presence.

"Ms Adams, what are you doing here?" I ask. "Do you know where you are? Do you know who I am?"

She tilts her head at me. "Of course I know who you are, Mr Loose."

She is the first to pronounce my last name correctly. I have little time to appreciate it. Her eyes are so sharp. This is not the look of a woman in shock. Her gaze is as clear as her voice. She looks at the letter in my hand.

"I see you have found my latest missive," she says, sounding quite pleased with herself.

I look at the letter, as if her words will begin to make more sense if I find I am holding something different.

"You are awfully quiet, Mr Loose," she continues, turning back to look at the yew tree. "It became more and more difficult to bring these little letters here. That Detective Sergeant started catching onto me. She came back yesterday to question me herself. She even found some of the notes that I had taken from the garbage that Tessa brings home with her on her cleaning days." Elizabeth Adams points outside, into the direction of the drive. "A shame, because it was so convenient. My house is just on the other side of the woods, as I am sure you are aware. All of this used to be my family's property. It was really just a quick evening stroll. Quite exciting, I have to say."

It takes me a moment to realise that I'm shaking my head. Elizabeth Adams must have spotted it. "Oh, you don't believe me, do you? Why is that, Mr Loose? Do you also believe that the elderly aren't capable of holding a rifle? Of professing their opinions? Or that they shouldn't be allowed to?" Her smile slowly vanishes. "I will have you know, Mr Loose, that the elderly are still alive, no matter how inconvenient to the young. I'm not dead yet. And I have no intention to relinquish my say over the matters of the country I love before I've been buried."

"Mrs Adams," I say. "Are you telling me that it was you who has been threatening Kate? That it was you, standing outside her house with a rifle, shattering her window with a brick?"

She does not reply directly, instead returning to her enigmatic smile. "You cannot be ignored when you are holding a rifle, Mr Loose. Isn't that right?"

Elizabeth Adams looks out of the window again. To the

view of the tree. "That tree," she goes on, "is part of our heritage." She stands up, straightens her skirt, then slowly walks away. I follow her through the kitchen and into the hall, then out of the front door. She is making for the tree. I follow her.

Standing in the cold and the snow, Elizabeth Adams puts one of her wrinkled hands onto the wrinkled bark of the tree. She holds on. "This tree will endure. It will stand here until the end of time, when all of us have long been forgotten. So will the yew in the graveyard. It will outlive us all."

"Mrs Adams," I repeat. "Was it you who sent those threatening letters to Kate?"

"Yes," she says, hand still on the bark. It's cold out, so cold. The air is grey and thick and silent. The light is pale. Fear is threading its way up my skin, crawling across my spine. The rowan tree and its thin, thin branches, winding their way back towards my lungs.

"Why?" I ask.

"Because she thought she was above the laws of this country," Elizabeth Adams says. "She thought she could do what she wanted and not fear punishment. But no one is above the law. The world may think differently, but we do not want the world's barbarity here."

"You found out about the abortion," I say.

"Kate O'Leary helped murder my grandchild," Elizabeth Adams says. "She took away my legacy."

"William told you that Alice's child was his."

She smiles benevolently. "He told me. He came to me after he'd done it. Manslaughter, of course. A crime of passion. I wonder how harshly a jury would have judged him." Elizabeth's expression darkens for a moment. "Alice Walsh asked him to come over, out of the blue. He was so worried, he left work straightaway. Her parents weren't there. She didn't want them to know. And there she told him she had murdered his child, without even consulting him, sitting on the bed where the sheets still carried the remnants of the blood that was proof of her crime. She told him, 'because she thought it was right he should know', now that the deed had already been done. Him, who had wanted children all his life."

Then she shakes her head. Looks me in the eye, holding my attention as if we were in court and she was imprinting something essential upon the jury. "He did not mean to kill her when he attacked her at first. It was clearly a crime of passion. He was distraught when he discovered she was dead. So distraught that he turned to me. It was me who cut up her body. Just like her foetus would have been cut up, when abortions still worked a little differently than they do today." She spreads her hands. "I was inspired by a case I once presided over as a judge, where a young man had left a woman behind in much the same state. Her name was Emily Ryan. He left her like this, and so did I leave Alice Walsh." Again she smiles at the yew tree. Gently. "If I could not leave this world a grandchild, I would leave it a message. I would leave it justice."

I stare at her. "Then it was you," I say. "The judge who presided over the Ryan case was you."

"Oh, you know about it?" There, that smile. It is proud. "I wanted to make sure to let everyone know that this is what you had coming when you killed your own child. Or when you helped kill a child. So that they would stop and think before they did anything like that. Those women. That was to be my legacy."

Elizabeth Adams reaches for something. Something has been hidden against the trunk of the dead tree, on the side that is turned away from the house.

It is an old pistol.

I raise both hands. "Mrs Adams…"

"Isn't it wonderful?" she says, chuckling at my expression, her eyes still hazy. "Isn't it wonderful how, the moment you pick up a pistol, you matter again? I gave Kate O'Leary fair warning. I gave fair warning to the both of you. I asked you to leave, Mr Loose. You did not."

"Mrs Adams, what good could it do to—"

"Do you know how many yew trees grow in Germany?" She lifts the pistol gently. "Four. A total of four." Her old arms are shaking, but at this distance, her aim will not have to be precise.

Both hands still lifted, I feel the branches of the rowan tree shoot through my lungs, my heart, wind their way thick and sharp through my body, cutting open all my sinews, my veins, my arteries. She won't hesitate. Not the woman who cut Alice Walsh to pieces. And there are a million things I haven't done yet. A million things. I haven't seen Kate again. I haven't apologised to Daniel. I haven't lived the life I saw ahead of me.

Elizabeth Adams cocks her pistol. She is still smiling that smile. This is how she can control me.

And in one second, in two, in three

She will kill me

She will end me

For all of a moment, she will control everyone who does not behave the way they ought to. The foreigner, the young woman who defied her, the doctor. For all of a moment, she will be in control of the world that has spun away from her.

"I gave you fair warning, Mr Loose," she says. "I told you to go home."

But I am at home when I'm with her, I want to say. I don't want to look at Elizabeth Adams as I take my last breath. I would rather be thinking of Kate. Of Daniel.

But then something catches my attention.

Over Elizabeth Adams's shoulder.

A silhouette.

Coming out of the grey insubstantial dawn. The fog has hidden their presence until they are so close that they can almost touch us.

They are holding a proper gun.

I know who it is.

Detective Inspector Adam Kwiatkowski has his gun raised.

"Do not shoot, Mrs Adams," he calls out. "Put down your weapon." His voice is so sharp it could cut the yew tree in half where we stand. Behind him, I see more officers emerge from the fog, led by Detective Sergeant Olivia Cahill.

Elizabeth Adams swallows. "This is my legacy," she says.

"Put down your weapon," Detective Inspector Kwiatkowski says. "Now."

"I will have a legacy," Elizabeth Adams insists. "This is what I leave behind."

"Step away from this man, Mrs Adams, and put down your weapon."

Elizabeth Adams sways.

Sways.

"It is a worthy legacy," she says quietly.

Then she lifts the pistol to her temple and pulls the trigger.

I'm back at the hospital. I tell the doctors what I need is to sleep for twenty-four hours and ask if there isn't anything they could do to help with that.

09:15

They oblige me.

STATEMENT

DETECTIVE SERGEANT OLIVIA CAHILL AND DETECTIVE
INSPECTOR ADAM KWIATKOWSKI INTERVIEWING SEAN
O'DOHERTY
19 MAIN STREET
BT34 3DY

We just meant to scare him. Of course we'd never have…
What a ludicrous idea. That we would hang someone from
a tree. It was meant to scare them. Seeing as you lot weren't
doing anything.

What do you mean, as an officer of the law? That is
exactly what I was trying to do. I was trying to uphold the
law. There still is a law against abortion in this country.

But you don't care about this at all, do you? For you, it's
all over now, isn't it? I had to keep us safe when you
wouldn't.

What do you mean, did my past relationship with Kate
O'Leary have anything to do with this? Do you think I was
jealous? Jealous of Father Daniel? A priest who sleeps
around? No, let me tell you. I had no reason to be jealous. I
was just trying to protect Kate. I'd been trying to protect her

from the start. We didn't know she was going to be at the rectory.

But she was so obstinate. Tried to tell me she didn't want my protection.

Fine, if she didn't want it, she wasn't going to get it.

No, seriously, tell me, what exactly did I do wrong? What did she think, that I was good enough to fuck, but not good enough to be with her? That she could have a bit of sex with me and then disappear from my life?

I don't hate women. I love women.

It isn't me. It's the women. They don't seem to like me. I'm not picky. I'm not fussy. I look fine. I work out, I wear cologne, I'm getting my haircuts at a real hairdresser's. And still.

I'm alone.

What? Am I not good enough for them?

But yeah, anyway. That isn't what we're here to talk about. We just meant to scare him, is all. We wanted to make sure Daniel Reid knew that he wasn't welcome anymore in Annacairn.

No, not for a second did I think he'd murdered her. He isn't the type, is he? All lanky like that.

But this wasn't about the murder. He lied to us. He encouraged Alice Walsh to break the law. And I knew you lot weren't going to do anything about it. I knew that there wasn't anything you could do. So I knew we had to scare him away. If we didn't scare him away, he would stay. Because you wouldn't be able to touch him. He'd stay and keep poisoning the minds of our children. And I'm responsible for this community. I have to keep them safe.

Because no one else is going to do it, are they? Look at Stormont. A fucking joke, that. And nobody in Westminster thinks of us. It's just the rich helping the rich.

Who kept Daniel Reid and Kate O'Leary safe? What do you mean when you say that?

Why do I get to decide who gets to stay safe and who doesn't, you ask?

I've lived there all my life. In Annacairn. My family's lived there for ever.

Who should decide if not me?

Day 7

_____

TUESDAY 8TH JANUARY 2019

STATEMENT
DETECTIVE SERGEANT OLIVIA CAHILL AND DETECTIVE
INSPECTOR ADAM KWIATKOWSKI INTERVIEWING ENDA
O'REILLY
2 COLLEGE RD
GLASHEEN
CORK
T12 ACP5

I am so sorry. So, so sorry.

For Beth and Liz.

Alice. We called her Liz. In Cork, during the summer. She wanted a change. She wanted to be someone else, I think. Maybe she was becoming someone else, too.

I watched the two of them, all summer, and I knew what was going on. I totally knew what my sister was thinking, anyway. It was painfully obvious. She'd never been so smitten with anyone.

And I thought Alice felt the same. And then we came here, and Liz told us that she had slept with that friend of her father's. And that it had backfired, massively, because she got pregnant. But that she had had an abortion.

So then we didn't know what to make of that. Beth didn't know what to make of that.

I thought she had done it basically to pray the gay away. And Liz wanted to talk to Beth about it. She was going to. That night. They were going to have dinner that night. I would have, dunno, gone for a really long walk or whatever.

I would have walked and walked and walked in the snow. I like walking in the snow.

But then they couldn't.

They never will now.

She's dead, isn't she? We will never know what she really wanted. We will never know if she loved my sister back.

They never had dinner. I never went for that walk. Betha never found out the truth.

She never will.

There is a hand intertwined with mine when I wake up. It feels familiar.

When I look up, it is into Kate's face. She is sitting by the side of my bed. We're alone. There is no sign of Daniel. My heart gives a tug as I realise that he isn't here, but then I look back at Kate. She's wearing her grey suit. The one she wears for comfort.

"Did they let you drive home just to get that?" I ask, looking back at the ceiling, just enjoying her presence and the feel of her hand in mine.

"Let me?" she asks, her voice scratchy. "I'd like to see them try and stop me."

"So would I," I say. "I have to say, though, they are very kind here. Whatever they gave me to help me go to sleep, it worked like a charm." I close my eyes, bathing in the warmth of the blanket and the after-effects of the drug. "I might still be dreaming, actually. Maybe I did get shot under the yew tree after all, and this is the afterlife."

Kate squeezes my hand. And then, to my surprise, I hear her giggle.

Offended, I open my eyes to glare at her. She is trying to keep a straight face but failing miserably.

"Oh, thank you very much," I say. "No, really, I'm touched."

"Sorry!" she calls out, letting go of my hand to cover her face in hers. "It's just so fucking absurd. We're so lucky that Daniel woke up when he did. Olivia interviewed him, and she hadn't forgotten about the threats. She was onto Elizabeth Adams already. When Daniel confirmed he'd seen her that night in the graveyard when I was hurt, she told Kwiatkowski. And then they learned you'd gone home. They made straight for the house. Arrived just in time."

So I was right. Daniel had been lying. I wonder what made him want to protect her.

She shakes her head. "And you said it from the start, didn't you? That it may have been a woman who hit me over the head. Bit fucking mad, that. Elizabeth Adams."

I turn back to the ceiling. "She wanted to keep the past alive for just a little bit longer. She even wanted to bring it back."

From the corner of my eye, I can tell that Kate is lowering her hands, sobering up very quickly. "I wish people would stop wanting to bring the past back in this country. Or that they'd at least not shoot each other over it."

We sit beside each other in silence. Words are difficult to come by. Kate runs a finger along the bed sheets, drawing a pattern on the white fabric that I can't decipher.

"I like to think that this country is different now. That it changed. And it has. But you know, it wasn't changed by the people who shot each other. It was changed by people who campaigned for civil rights, for women's rights, for marriage equality. By the people who pushed back the influence of the church." Kate's fingers still. "When I was a child, there were so many decisions that society made for you, that you couldn't make on your own. Now, this is so different."

I cannot help but think of Alice Walsh. It was not so

different for her. When she made a decision of her own, she was murdered. And Kate was nearly murdered over it, too.

So was I.

"Is it different?"

Kate nods fervently. "It is. It is. And we'll know how to defend our rights when it comes to it."

"How?" I ask. "When they turn up with guns at your practice, at a clinic?"

"By not being afraid," she said.

"I was afraid," I admit quietly. "I was afraid to die."

"Aye," she says. "Me too."

I remember her on her knees in the graveyard. Remember the black cloth going over her head, swallowing up her face, as if she had never existed. As if she had already ceased to exist. Like Alice Walsh. Alice Walsh, who no longer exists. Alice Walsh, the only one of the three of us who had her whole life ahead of her still.

"It is about not letting fear stop you, then," Kate says.

I cannot help but reach for her hand again. She's so brave. She has always been able to look the truth in the eye. I could never do it quite as well as her.

"You are right," I say. Because she is. And I decide that I would rather be fearless, too. "Did I ever tell you," I go on, even though the words will barely come. "Did I ever tell you that I have wanted to kiss you for years?" There it sits. The truth. "Just to kiss you. Nothing else."

She looks at me.

"Not that that matters," I hurry to add. "It's all right. I just didn't see what the point was of keeping it from you."

She leans up to kiss me.

It's just what I thought it would be. It's a kiss, and it is easy and honest and after a few moments she is grinning a little and then I am laughing, and God, I have wanted to do this for so long. We separate, and Kate sits back down, still smiling.

"Thank you," she says after a long moment of silence.

I shake my head. "What for?"

"Well," she says, turning towards me, a small smile on her face. "For being on my side. For not leaving me alone."

"Nah," I say. "It's nothing."

She buries her face against my upper arm for a moment. "You got shot at for your troubles," she says, her voice suspiciously throaty.

"Were you worried?" I ask, because I want to make her smile.

She likes the way I say "worried". It is the only word I routinely mispronounce. It's even worse when it is preceded by "very".

She grins against my arm. "Very. And you?"

"Very, very worried," I repeat.

She intertwines her fingers with mine once more. Then she sits up and looks out of the window.

That is how we stay for a long, long while. The truth is smiling contentedly at the back of my mind. It is satisfied, for now.

Although there is one last thing, it whispers to me. It is not just that I have not found Daniel yet, have not spoken to him yet, have not seen him whole and hale. No, the truth is whispering

Do you feel that?

And that is the moment that I do feel it. Kate's shoulders are shaking.

She is crying.

And thank God, because so am I.

We are safe.

We got away.

For a few more years, we got away.

On our way home, we make three stops: one at the hardware store, one at the florist's, and one at the supermarket. Once at home, we finally board up the bedroom window to the best of our abilities, and the result isn't half bad. Then we get the slips of paper we collected in the church, tie each around a single white rose, and put them in water until we can take them to Alice Walsh's memorial, to the graveyard.

And then we make dinner.

Sauté potatoes with caramel and dried plums, one of the best winter dishes I know. I cut and season the potatoes with salt and rosemary while Kate melts the sugar. I put on my music. She starts swaying her hips, standing in front of the oven. I finish seasoning the potatoes and make my way to the sink to wash my hands. Under no circumstances would I say that I was dancing across the room.

Except maybe I am. Kate laughs at me, rightfully so. I take my revenge by wiping off my salty rosemary hands on her suit jacket. She shrieks. Actually shrieks. And then I'm the one who is shrieking, because she has jabbed her fingers into my sides and that is entirely unfair, because I unwisely revealed to her where I was ticklish one drunk night fifteen years ago in Australia and she still remembers.

Then we go back to being real people, and I start making Knickerbocker Glory with crystallised pecans, from scratch. I watch the raspberries turn soft and mushy as I puree them by hand, their juice red and sweet as I lick it off my fingers.

I smell the sharp scent of the lemon and feel the burn of its juice on the cuts on my hand. The powdered sugar is soft and light and white, as soft as the dried plums and as white as the sea salt and the snow outside on the ground and in the trees and in the sky.

I don't know what it is about food, except that it reminds you that you are alive.

When the potatoes are in the oven, sizzling in caramel and salt and rosemary, and the semifreddo in the freezer, turning sugar and lemon juice and raspberries into ice cream, I try not to look at Kate as I ask, as if it did not matter much either way: "Should we ask Daniel to join us, or would you prefer we didn't?"

I determine to pretend that I don't see how she rolls her eyes at me in exasperated fondness before handing me the phone. "He should be out walking. Might mean you get lucky, and that he has a signal."

I listen to the ringing sounds on the line. There is sinking feeling at the bottom of my stomach.

Daniel's voice is scratchy when he answers. Scratchy, and guarded.

"This is Jannis," I say.

An intake of breath.

Nothing else.

"Would you like to come over for tea?" I ask. And pray. Properly pray. In my head, begging God to be good to me.

It is the first time in years.

Daniel is perfectly punctual.

We sit at the kitchen table, the three of us, and we eat and drink, and all the while, I can't take my eyes off of him.

After dessert, Kate does something very kind. She rises, stretches, and says: "Right. I will go and sit outside now and pretend to look at the stars, and you two talk."

And then she leaves, and it's just the two of us.

Daniel huffs out a laugh. "Subtle."

I shrug. I'm nervous.

So nervous.

He looks at me. He's wearing a grey sweater and grey jeans with black sneakers. He doesn't say anything else.

"We tied each message to a rose," I say, pointing helplessly at the roses standing in buckets of water throughout the kitchen. "We want to take them to the memorial. Later. If we can work up the nerve, that is."

He nods.

Still, he doesn't say anything.

"You saw her in the graveyard, didn't you?" I ask quietly. "You saw Elizabeth Adams in the graveyard, when Kate was hit over the head."

Slowly, Daniel shakes his head. "Just her car. Then I found it too difficult to credit that she would have anything to do with it. I just thought that William or Tessa had driven her home that afternoon, and she'd left her car. I told the police when they questioned me in the hospital. Just in time, it seems."

I nod.

"Do you know," he says after a moment's silence, "it was her who gave me the Tesla. She said she needed something smaller, something slower, with her eyesight fading. I wonder if that was true. Or if she simply wanted me indebted to her. If she did, it worked. I should have told the police right away."

Another silence.

"You will have to move away, I suppose," I say instead.

"Yes," Daniel replies. "Just like you will have to catch a plane and go back home. But that isn't what Kate left us to talk about, is it?"

I look at him. Still sitting there. Hands folded in his lap.

And is that an innocent smile I see on his face?

Tentatively, I smile back. "Who said anything about talking?"

I have a bit of an uncompromising relationship with the truth, you see. I do not wine it dine it take it to bed. I tell it.

But him? I would very much like to do all of that to him.

"There's a flight at 7:15."

"In the morning?"

"Yep."

"Too early. Far too early. Isn't there one in the evening? Late? I could take you out to dinner in Belfast. That place where they serve vegan fish and chips."

"The one on Ann Street?"

"Yes, that one. You know, the cute one."

"What was its name again?"

"Fish Town?"

"Fish City!"

"Yes, Fish City! That's it!"

Kate and I are in the living room, bent over her laptop, looking at flights out of Belfast. I'm swaying gently to the music that's on in the background. She is redoing her nails.

Outside, the rowan trees scratch along the walls. They tap against the window. The wind is ruffling their branches. It makes them whisper.

Inside, the room is warm and bright as I look at her. "Did I really flirt with the bartender, back in Seventeen Seventy-Seven?"

She finishes off her pinky with a flourish. Red is the colour of choice. "God, yes."

"Was I any good?"

"Well, I think it didn't help your case that you were also flirting with me."

I shake my head. "Sorry about that."

337

"Don't be," she says. "We were very young."

"Still," I continue. "You deserve better. Much better than the men you've been getting, Kate."

Kate looks up at me. Red nails, red dressing gown. "Well, I picked them, didn't I?"

She puts away the nail polish and leans back into the couch. We listen to the music and the branches scratching at the window and the whispers of the wind.

"I wonder at that," she says suddenly. "Why I kept choosing men who didn't really want me."

I make to protest, but she waves it away.

"And places, too." She motions around, indicating, I presume, Annacairn. "I thought I was doing what was right, coming to practise here. I was naïve."

I look out at the yew tree. "You had the best intentions."

"Ah, that may be true." She shrugs. Looks out at the yew tree, too. It is an evergreen tree. "But what good are those?"

"Road to hell and all that?"

"Pretty literal in this case, wasn't it? Nearly got killed under a yew tree."

We fall silent for a while. We are still looking at the tree outside. Still listening to the wind.

Then Kate speaks up again: "Maybe all I was looking for was a fight, really."

"What do you mean?"

"The men. This place. Maybe all I wanted was to have something to fight for. Something to fight against."

"Is it such a bad thing, being a fighter?"

She smiles. Stares at the snow, white on the ground.

White in the bright light of the moon. "Maybe not. But is it such a bad thing, either, to just be happy?"

I think of Daniel as I look at the snow myself. How the moonlight makes it glow and glimmer, how beautiful the Mourne Mountains are. How beautiful Annacairn, its church and its graveyard are.

I think of how we were all nearly killed not one day ago.

And then I think of Alice Walsh.

"No," I say. "You're right. It really isn't such a bad thing, just being happy."

We look at each other. Then I smile at her. "Still, I like that you're a fighter."

She laughs. "I like that I'm a fighter, too."

Another silence stretches out between us. The night outside is noisier than this room, even with the music on. Trees are creaking. Branches are rustling. Animals are out in the woods, out in the snow. I turn back to the list of flights. Scroll down.

"Look, there's one at nine."

"In the morning?" Kate asks, absent-mindedly.

"In the evening."

"Perfect. Make a booking." Then she grins at me, turning her gaze away from the snow and the moon and the tree. "And don't forget to leave Daniel your number."

I laugh and go to fetch my credit card.

I've made the booking and put away the laptop. Kate is still sitting on the couch. She is looking out of the window again, at the yew tree outside, in the snow, under the light of the moon. The music has gone out. Branches are tapping at the windows. Scratching against the wall. Creaking. Crackling.

"I'll miss the house," she says. "I'll miss the garden."

The garden that lies still under the light of the moon and the stars. The garden that speaks and whispers. The garden that is alive, even at night.

"Where you will go?" I ask. "You will have to go, won't you? Give up the practice."

"Yes, of course. Innocent or not, the local whispers won't die down." She shrugs. "Maybe the other side of the Mourne Mountains is far enough. Or Dublin. Or, you know, Germany! Germany's lovely, isn't it?"

"You're always welcome," I say, joining her.

She smiles gently, still looking out of the window. "Yes, I know."

"Your parents are in Dublin, aren't they?"

"Close by."

"Right."

Kate nods. As if to a thought she has had. Then she looks at me. Looks away from the moon and the tree and the snow.

"Wherever it is I go," she says, "it will be somewhere that I am wanted."

341

Then she grins. "I've always liked Australia, myself."

I raise my brows. "Australia, yes?"

She laughs. "Think about it! No snow. No yew trees. Lovely pub in Newcastle, by the Queen's Wharf. Lots of beachgoers, too. Shirtless, all of them. Handsome views, they say."

"This time, don't pick the one who flirts with the bartender, too," I say. "It's just poor taste."

She smiles at me. "Very true. But I was tempted, you know."

"Back then?"

"Of course. I liked you. I thought it might be fun to go home with you. And there was something very alluring about your voice. The way you said it. Let me drive you home. I'll always remember that."

"And I'll always remember what you answered," I say. "'I'm not scared'."

Kate nods.

And then she says: "You know what?"

"What?"

"That was a lie." She looks at me, legs stretched out in front of her, arms behind her head. It is warm in this room, and bright. "Back in Newcastle, when we first met, that was a lie. It was the fighter in me. Refusing to be scared even though I was. Scared of what might happen to me out walking, on the way home, clutching my keys, holding my phone to my ear, pretending to be talking to someone. Scared of what might happen to me, taking home a man I didn't know to have sex with. Scared of admitting I was scared."

"And now?" I ask.

She smiles at me. Lowers her arms as she grins. "Now I'm brave enough to admit that I'm scared. It's a scary thing, life, isn't it?"

I think of standing across from Daniel in the sacristy, pulling him close. I think of speaking the truth and what it costs. I think of Alice Walsh. And then I think of Kate, how she knelt in the snow on the graveyard, a bag over her head. How I thought the yew tree was laughing at me. Creaking. Crackling. I look out at the tree in her garden, where I was threatened, where Elizabeth Adams took her life.

"Yes," I say.

"And a bit of a miracle," she adds.

I am still looking at the yew tree. Even in the winter, it does not look bare. It does not look dead. Its leaves are green, and spring will come, and then it will be warm again outside, warm and bright.

But I know that that is an illusion. In the spring, leaves will grow. It will be green, bright green, and it will be warm outside, warm and bright.

I put my head on her shoulder, looking out at the yew tree, at the snow so bright in the light of the moon. I listen to the whispers of the wind. To her breath and mine. I think of eating fish and chips with her at Fish City in Belfast tomorrow. I think of giving Daniel my number before I leave. I think of visiting her at her new practice, in Dublin, in Germany, in Australia. Where the sun shines bright and warm and the bartenders are handsome and where I met a friend for life when I had least expected it.

"Yes," I say. "It is a bit of a miracle."

EVIDENCE #10662
CATEGORY: E-MAIL, VICTIM
STATUS: NOT SENT
DESCRIPTION:
THE LAST E-MAIL DRAFTED BY ALICE WALSH.

Betha,

I want to tell you something. I just don't have the words to do so. I think I don't have the words because we don't talk much in my family. There is still so much shame. So many things we don't discuss. Normal things. A woman's period. Sex. Death.

Peace.

Sometimes I feel like my dad is ashamed that there is peace now. As if peace meant that he had lost.

I don't think I ever told you, not you, not Enda, because it isn't a thing you tell people, but Dad was arrested during the Troubles. Mum thinks he was tortured at Ballykelly. But we don't talk about that, either. As if it was another thing to be ashamed of. Getting tortured.

And we don't talk about how my mum didn't want me before I was born. We don't talk about how my dad made her have me. And how I think he shouldn't have done that, even though of course I want to be here. I want to be alive.

We don't talk about that child that was growing inside of me.

I remember that my mum and I were best friends. When I was a child, she was my best friend. Could I have been the best friend to this child? Was I the only one this kid had, and I got rid of it?

Did I make a mistake, Betha?

Maybe. But at least I had a choice.

It's crazy, isn't it? I take it all for granted. That I can have sex with whomever I want and that I can love whomever I want and that I can decide what to do with my body and that I can go be a doctor or a journalist or a mechanical engineer if I want.

And peace. Peace especially. I just take it for granted, but it's not.

Is it going to get worse?

I want it to get better.

I want to be better.

I want to be better with you, Beth.

If you want that, too. If you want to be with me. Preferably for ever, because I'm in love with you.

Or at least till the end. Because of course it has to end at some point. I realised that just the other day.

There will be an end to life one day. But there are many, many years ahead, and it will get better. It is already better. I can love whomever I want. Be with whomever I want. I have the right.

It's our future, and it will be glorious.

Just you wait.

Acknowledgments

I would like to thank the Society of Authors and the Author's Foundation for the grant that enabled me to travel to Northern Ireland in 2020 as part of the research for this novel.

My heartfelt thanks go out to Jolene, who was kind enough to come talk to me in Belfast over Afternoon Tea, and to Clara Clasen, for connecting us.

Many thanks also to Gareth and Emma from the gorgeous Mourne Country House who were the most generous hosts we could have wished for.

I would also like to thank the very nice man I met at Waterstones Newry standing before the history section, from which sprung an enlightening conversation about history, politics, racism, capitalism and the future of Nothern Ireland. My thanks also go out to the staff of that Waterstones, who were very attentive.

In general, I was welcomed with the greatest warmth, and everyone was incredibly generous with their time; I could not have wished for kinder people or a lovelier time when researching this book in Ireland.

As always, and in this instance in particular, I owe a great debt of gratitude to my agent, Thérèse Coen, who always bears my conduct with the greatest grace and patience, even during a global pandemic. I also thank Caroline, Jo, Hannah, and Nicole, the brilliant team at Hardman & Swainson Literary Agency.

Thank you also to Bethan, Charlotte, and the equally brilliant team at One More Chapter: for your time, your patience, for pushing me to make this the best book it could be – and for the most beautiful cover art!

Thank you to Tony for a conscientious copyedit revealing critical information – such as that yew trees are evergreens.

I would like to thank my colleagues: Verena, Michi, Mitja, Maria, Jens, Tom, Charlotte, and the students of the Novel Writing Workshop at the University of Bonn. I would also like to thank Stefan Plasa and Marion Gymnich from the University of Bonn, for believing in me before I'd earned it.

Thank you, always, to Nils, Matthias, Laura, dad, mum. Thank you, mum, for coming on this research trip with me, and showing me how to have a good time.

YOUR NUMBER ONE STOP

ONE MORE CHAPTER

FOR PAGETURNING BOOKS

One More Chapter is an
award-winning global
division of HarperCollins.

Sign up to our newsletter to get our
latest eBook deals and stay up to date
with our weekly Book Club!
<u>Subscribe here.</u>

Meet the team at
<u>www.onemorechapter.com</u>

Follow us!
🐦 <u>@OneMoreChapter_</u>
📘 <u>@OneMoreChapter</u>
📷 <u>@onemorechapterhc</u>

Do you write unputdownable fiction?
We love to hear from new voices.
Find out how to submit your novel at
<u>www.onemorechapter.com/submissions</u>